Carl Weber's Kingpins:

New Orleans

Carl Weber's Kingpins:

New Orleans

Randy Coxton

www.urbanbooks.net

Urban Books, LLC
300 Farmingdale Road, NY-Route 109
Farmingdale, NY 11735

Carl Weber's Kingpins: New Orleans

ISBN 13: 978-1-64556-621-2

First Mass Market Printing June 2024
First Trade Paperback Printing August 2023
Printed in the United States of America

10 9 8 7 6 5 4 3 2 1

Distributed by Kensington Publishing Corp.
Submit Orders to:
Customer Service
400 Hahn Road
Westminster, MD 21157-4627
Phone: 1-800-733-3000
Fax: 1-800-659-2436

Prologue

When Fire Meets Ice

Freeway was looking forward to his meeting with Belladonna. He needed a new plug, and word around town was she was the connect of the French Quarter. She was a part of the Gambino Family. The Gambinos ran the French Quarter. Anyone doing business in the Quarter had to deal with them. Freeway's plug had just got knocked on RICO charges. He and Belladonna ran in the same circles but never dealt with each other. Their initial meeting was pretty rocky. Freeway thought she was a bitch, and she thought he was a control freak. Both were apprehensive of the other's motives.

Freeway stood at the bar, puffing on a cigar. The cigars were Cuban and were a guilty pleasure he picked up while in the military. He loved the smell of pipe tobacco, and since he'd look crazy as hell smoking a pipe, he found the same taste and texture in a cigar.

Freeway was not an avid smoker, but there was something about a good cigar pairing with the right liquor. He was a bit of a snob when it came to a good cigar. Freeway owed that tutelage to his granddad, but everybody had their vices. His were a nice ass and a good cigar.

Freeway was old school. What he smoked, he learned from the best. His grandfather was one of the few who escaped Castro's regime and pressed his way to Atlanta, then on to New Orleans. He was 18 at the time of the revolution and was one of only a few Afro Cubans who left. Augusto knew there had to be more than working in the tobacco fields, so he took his chances in the New World.

Most of his life had been around tobacco in some form or fashion. Starting as a young child, he had been a field hand working in tobacco fields. Augusto started picking tobacco, then moved on to working in the curing houses. Some bails would sit for years curing to make the perfect cigar. Augusto showed a talent for understanding which leaves were the best for curing and was soon trained at an early age to work in the primary house at the farm, where they had rooms dedicated to those that selected the leaves to roll the perfect Cuban cigar. Augusto was, if nothing else . . . patient, another trait that Freeway inherited from his grandfather, and absorbed all he knew. Augusto bided his time and took that craft with him when he left Cuba.

Augusto taught Freeway a lot, and one of the most important things he learned was that things were never as simple as they seemed on the surface. That advice saved him many a day when Freeway served in the marines. Take, for instance, the cigar he was smoking. The posh hotel club Freeway was sitting in claimed that the cigar he was smoking was imported from Cuba. Freeway could tell by the taste that this was anything *but* a genuine Cuban cigar. They had three leaves that made the filler: ligero, vilado, and seco. Depending on the flavor you want, you'd add more or less ligero. Freeway preferred spicy, so heavy ligero was a must. What he was smoking was a nice knockoff, but definitely *not* Cuban.

Freeway had been in the French Quarter longer than expected. There was trouble brewing in the 7th Ward, and he needed to get his shit together before he returned. Well, that and the fact that the competition needed to be scoped out.

Business comes first, though. The new connect on Bourbon Street had been named, but none of that would matter if they couldn't get this small problem resolved. Freeway was successful since no one knew he existed. He prided himself on his lack of attention. It helped him move seamlessly in both worlds. However, the Gambinos were making it hard to remain invisible. Time was running out, though. Freeway would need to press his way back to the Ward soon and tell his crew what he had found.

Belladonna was another matter. It wasn't a mystery that she now had feelings for Freeway, at least not to Freeway anyway, but Belladonna was still trying to play both sides. With Freeway's line of work, a relationship was a weak spot. The reality was that Freeway was ready to settle down, and Belladonna was the one. She just needed to be convinced that she was the one. This Sukie chick, though, was trouble . . . and also her sister.

Freeway had been following Sukie for several days. Sukie was a distraction but had ties to her father. One thing that Freeway knew was that Sukie was not all that she appeared to be. If any man thought they were the only one fucking her, they were sadly mistaken. Freeway didn't have any direct proof she was laying up with someone else, but that dude taking her home from classes? Freeway knew "Lame Boy" when he saw it.

Freeway was really in the French Quarter for two purposes. One was Belladonna, and the other was to get a line of sight on who dared mess with the business flow of his empire. Several businesses had been hit, both legally and illegally. He had to run down what he could find directly on-site. What Freeway found was interesting. The Gambino clique was small but efficient and racked up quite a lot from his business and other business partners.

They just needed a name, and the Gambinos were the ones that kept being mentioned.

Freeway was flipping through the intel he had just received via phone. Sipping on Cognac and puffing on the bogus cigar, he read through the massive losses from last night. It appears that one club alone was hit for two hundred thousand.

Shit, I guess the problem wasn't so small, Freeway thought.

It had to be an inside job because they were in and out too quickly. Ignorance was bliss, and right now, these clowns were happy as hell. So sad they won't have long to enjoy their ill-gotten gain. Change was coming, and Freeway needed distractions to be minimal. Just as those thoughts popped into his head, a text came through with one word—Lucky.

Belladonna sashayed into the bar wearing a blue Dolce & Gabbana dress with red and blue Manolo pumps. Freeway smiled at her presence. He was surprised she was there without a bodyguard, so he was sure she was packing. He stood as she got close.

He extended his hand and said, "It's a pleasure to meet you, Miss Gambino."

She smiled as she took in his looks as well.

"No, the pleasure is all mine," she said as he pulled out her chair.

"Thank you. I see that you are a gentleman," she said.

"Yeah, my mama taught me a little something," responded Freeway.

As Belladonna looked over the drink menu, Freeway lusted over her beauty.

"So, what can I get you to drink?" asked Freeway.

"I'll have a Jack on the Rocks," she answered.

"Oh, I expected you to drink some fruity drink," he joked.

"That's a nice suit you're wearing," Belladonna complimented him.

"It's a Dolce & Gabbana," he replied. Something about Freeway's eyes had Belladonna captivated.

After a round of drinks, Freeway asked, "Are we going to fuck or do business?"

Belladonna's mouth fell open at his comment.

"Well, I see our manners have gone out the window," she smiled as she chewed on a cherry.

"No sense in wasting each other's time," Freeway smiled.

"I'm definitely not the type of girl that fucks on the first meeting," she answered.

"Let's get down to business then. I need a supplier, and I heard you're the person to see," he smirked. Belladonna reached for her purse as she stood.

"So, I'm assuming we're *not* doing business?" inquired Freeway.

"Let's go. I'll show you our operation," winked Belladonna.

"So, I'm assuming we're not doing business?" inquired Freeway again.

"I'm going to take option number two," flirted Belladonna.

"I have a room upstairs."

She smiled as Freeway gulped his drink and stood.

Freeway interlocked his arm with hers as they walked to his room. Minutes later, they stepped off the elevator. Freeway's room was at the end of the floor. They both were immersed in conversation.

"This is my room. You sure you ready for this?" he abruptly asked.

Belladonna smirked at his statement. As they entered the room, he pinned her to the door. Placing his lips to hers, he kissed her softly. Belladonna released a soft moan as their hands roamed each other's bodies. She put her hands on his chest as he kissed her neck.

"You sure you want to mix business with pleasure?" she moaned as her hand slid over his dick through his slacks.

Caught in the moment, he said, "I'm playing for keeps. Can't we do both?" Freeway's hand rested lightly on Belladonna's ass as he palmed it, looking into her eyes. He slightly raised her dress as he spun her around. His hands roamed over her breasts through the fabric.

"So, are we going to fuck or not?" whined Belladonna as she started pulling her dress over her head.

"Well, damn," Freeway said sarcastically. Belladonna stood with her arms in her plum-colored Keylove Victoria's Secret laced lingerie set. Freeway licked his lips as his eyes roamed every inch of her luscious body. Then tapping her foot and getting impatient, Belladonna whined, "Get undressed."

Freeway unbuttoned his shirt to reveal his inked-up chest. He moved in closer as he slid Bella's bra strap down her shoulder and lightly kissed it. She unfastened his slacks to reveal his long dick pressing to get out of his Calvin Klein boxers. Freeway's tongue latched on her hardened nipple as she slowly stroked his dick, moaning as he removed her panties.

"Get on the bed," he ordered with a half smile.

Lying back on the bed, he softly kissed her lips and trailed soft kisses on her body until he reached her pussy. Belladonna's eyes rolled in the back of her head as he gently ran his tongue over her clit.

"Oh, damn. Yes, daddy," she gasped as she moved her pussy back and forth over his tongue.

She grabbed his shoulders as her first climax rocked her to the core. Then gasping, she let out a slight sigh as he slid into her. Belladonna's eyes widened as her pussy adjusted to his size.

"Hold . . . Hold up," she moaned, pressing the palm of her hand into his chest.

"Nah, take this dick, you little spoiled ass," he mugged as he slid deeper into her pussy. Freeway picked up his pace, stroking in and out of her as she closed her eyes and dug her nails into his back, which only made him fuck her harder.

"Shiit," he yelped as he came.

Covered with sweat, he rolled off and lay beside her, winded. He side-eyed her, then joked, "So, are we doing business now?" Belladonna's body was still shaking.

Minutes later, she said, "Yes, daddy. I will make it happen," she cooed.

Chapter 1

Energy

Five Years Later . . .

Belladonna stepped out of the shower. As water dripped off her chocolate body, Freeway could only admire his lady. He took a sip of wine and set the glass on the dresser. Then he grabbed the towel off the bed he had waiting for her. He lightly kissed her on the forehead. She pulled off his shirt and whispered in his ear as she snatched the towel out of his hand.

"You still thinking about going out tonight?" She licked his earlobe.

"Maybe, why you ask?"

"I want you to stay home. Do you love me or those streets?"

"You know I love you. Don't do that."

"Prove it!" She unbuckled his belt and unzipped his pants.

Freeway always had money on his mind. Even though he ran a very lucrative illegal empire, he kept thinking of different ways to make more money. However, when it came to Belladonna, his thoughts of money instantly stopped. As she rubbed his chest, his heart began to beat fast. He picked her up and laid her on the bed. Then he sucked on her breasts, twirling his tongue around her nipples. She let out a fresh breath like clouds wrapping around a forbidden mountain. Finally, he slid his tongue down to her inner thigh.

"Freeway, I need you inside me, please," she screamed with anticipation.

"How bad you want me?" He dropped his Polo jeans to the floor while pushing his tongue deep inside her, feeling all her moisture.

Belladonna wrapped her legs around his neck, pushing her pussy closer to his face. His tongue grinded on her clit. She was so close to reaching her climax that he snatched her legs open, thrusting his manhood inside her. She screamed out to God, reaching for her pillows, screaming even louder now. Belladonna rotated her hips, fucking Freeway back the way only she could. The wetter her pussy got from his strokes, the weaker Freeway got. Finally, he unloaded all his juices inside her, yelling he loved her. Then he collapsed over her body, breathing heavily. Their energy was so amazing. It was like they shared the same heartbeat. Soon, Freeway rolled over, feeling so amazed. So many years together, and the sex was still explosive.

"So, you still going out?" She ran her fingers through his long dreads.

"Boo, you do this every time. You know I got an empire to run." Freeway exhaled for the conversation he was about to have.

"Yes, you do have an empire, an empire that's worth $405 million. I don't understand why you're still doing this." Belladonna jumped off the bed and headed for her walk-in closet.

"I'm making sure you don't have to want for nothing ever." Freeway began to put his clothes back on.

Belladonna was in the closet, not really looking for clothes. Instead, she was hiding the tears rolling down her face. She never wanted to look weak in front of her man. The way he saw her meant everything to her.

Freeway called her name twice. She quickly grabbed her plush Ralph Lauren robe that Freeway had paid to be made for her. When she walked out of the closet, Freeway knew she had been crying.

"Come on, Belladonna, why you crying?"

"I'm not crying." She quickly wiped her eyes.

"Now, you know there is something I know better than money, and that's you."

"Tell me the truth, Freeway. Do you love your money and empire more than me?"

"Why would you ask me that?"

"Just answer my question, dammit." Belladonna sat on the bed and crossed her arms.

Freeway was going to answer her, but right before he did, his doorbell rang. He told her to hold on, but she wasn't feeling it. She rolled her eyes as Freeway went downstairs to answer the door. When he opened the door, his right-hand man, Jackal, stood there. Jackal was second in command to the empire Freeway built. Besides Belladonna, Jackal was the only other person Freeway trusted. However, Freeway was not happy to see him right now. Boy, was his timing terrible.

"Nigga, I thought I told you I would meet you at the club."

"I know, but we got something important that came up."

"So?" Freeway didn't see his point.

"What you mean 'so'? You know niggas want the empire we built."

"Jackal, what's the point of you being the second in command if you can't conduct business without me?" Freeway felt frustrated.

"Why do you have to question my authority?" Jackal hated when his partner talked down to him this way.

"Look, go back to the club, and I'll meet you there." Freeway shut the door in Jackal's face without waiting for his response.

Then he went back upstairs. He had to get Belladonna straight so he could leave the house and handle business. This would not be an easy task. When he reached the bedroom, he noticed Belladonna was talking with her friend Asia. Freeway did not like Asia at all. He felt she was too reckless and loose with her body. She took no responsibility for the way she lived. Belladonna saw the frown on Freeway's face and hung up the phone.

"What did I tell you about that girl?"

"Don't go there, Freeway. I don't say shit about your low-life partner, Jackal."

"That's different."

"How is that?" She felt like Freeway was just making excuses.

"That's my business partner. Without him, I would not have built our empire."

"Whatever. I'm about to go out to a birthday party."

Freeway was changing his clothes and stopped buttoning up his red Dolce & Gabbana shirt when he heard Belladonna was going out. He thought it was ironic that she made that big fuss about him leaving because things had changed since she had been invited out to a party. Freeway had to protect her at all costs, considering who he was. He was not going to allow anybody to use her as his weakness.

"I sure hope this party is at my club."

"Actually, it's not. It's at Asia's homeboy's club." Belladonna braced herself because she knew her man was about to snap.

"Have you lost your damn mind, Belladonna?"

"What?" She got off the bed to put on her sundress and Red Bottom high heels.

"You know damn well what. You know that's Rozay's club, and you know that nigga been wanting my spot." Freeway was furious that his girl would think this recklessly.

"Baby, chill out. Rozay is out of town."

"I don't see how you can be friends with a bitch who hangs around a man I'm beefing with."

"Me and Asia have nothing to do with you and Rozay's beef, so please, leave us out of it."

Even though Freeway knew Asia didn't get along with Rozay that well, he still didn't trust the idea, but he did have business to handle tonight. When it came to his empire, he couldn't let anything get in the way. He knew he had to let it slide that Belladonna was going to his rival's club tonight. First, however, he was going to put down some ground rules.

"Look, I need you back at this house by midnight." He grabbed his gun and tucked it under his shirt.

"Freeway, I love you but don't you dare give me commands like that. I'll be back home when the party is over."

"Belladonna, you can get fly out of the mouth all you want to. But don't be the reason why some nigga get they head knocked off."

Belladonna knew her man didn't play any games when it came to her. It bothered her and turned her on at the same time. They both walked outside together and headed for the two-door garage where their cars were parked. Both drove Range Rovers. Freeway's car was red, and Belladonna's was black. Freeway refused to let her leave with an attitude. So, he walked over to make things right as a man should.

"Belladonna, I love you. Just be safe." He kissed her on the forehead.

"I will, but you never answered my question."

"What's that?"

"Do you love me or your empire?" This was a question she desperately needed an answer to.

"Belladonna, now is not the time, please." Freeway got into his car and drove off.

Belladonna was curious that he couldn't answer the question. Finally, she got into her car and headed to the club to meet Asia. Tonight, she was going to put all the negative bullshit out of her mind and enjoy herself. For once, she wasn't going to think about Freeway . . . just herself. She loved her soul mate, but it wasn't about him tonight. She thought one day, he would learn to get his priorities straight.

As Freeway drove, he rolled down his window to feel the cool New Orleans night breeze. He couldn't believe Belladonna had the nerve to ask that question again. He didn't just build the empire for himself. He was doing it for her too. He knew she was spoiled, but damn, that question was an insult to his intelligence.

Freeway pulled up to the club he owned. As soon as he parked, Jackal made his way to the car. He had been waiting the last hour for his partner to arrive.

"Damn, it's about time," Jackal expressed his anxiety.

"Nigga, calm down." Freeway rolled up his window and got out of the vehicle.

"Despite what you got going on at home, this is important."

"My household is important too. If it's so important, why didn't you handle it?"

"Look, we both decided not to make decisions without the other present."

"Well, you should have postponed whatever this bullshit is."

They both walked together into the club. The music was hitting the ceiling, and the drinks were being poured and served. Money was definitely on the club tonight. The DJ announced Freeway's name every time he entered the club. Freeway and Jackal were highly respected, but Freeway was always recognized first. Low-key Jackal was constantly jealous of that. Freeway was still trying to figure out what was so important that he had to be at the club tonight.

"Look, man, why am I here?" Freeway walked to the bar while waiting on an answer.

"Somebody wants to buy our empire again."

"Jackal, really, you know how I feel about selling my empire."

"I know, but this time, it's different."

"How is that?" Freeway received his D'ussé from the bar.

"They offering us five hundred million. That's almost eighty million profit."

"Who the fuck would offer us that much?" Freeway felt the offer was very suspicious.

"Before I tell you, you need to have a sound mind about this."

"Jackal, now, you got me wondering about *your* choices," smirked Freeway.

They headed to the VIP section that was made just for them. Bottles of the finest liquor were on the table, hot women were present, and a thick red rope blocked off the room. Freeway always wondered why women were in his section. He cared nothing for them. He was faithful to Belladonna.

She owned his heart, and he was fine with that. They entered the section and sat at the table set up for them. Freeway leaned over and whispered in Jackal's ear.

"Get these fucking women out of my section now. We about to do business. They don't need to be here." Freeway was very particular about who was around when he did business.

"OK, on it." Jackal signaled to the bouncer to get rid of the women.

The bouncer rounded up the women and told them they had to go. They were all upset. They felt important dancing in the VIP around Freeway and Jackal, but they also knew how Freeway felt about Belladonna. All of New Orleans knew that he was faithful to her.

"Promise you'll keep an open mind about this deal?" Jackal was trying to prepare Freeway for their business meeting.

"Why?"

"Because here he comes." Jackal stood up to get ready to greet their guest.

When Freeway saw who walked into his VIP section, he pulled his gun out and cocked it.

"Get the fuck out of my club, Rozay—right now." Then angrily, Freeway pointed his gun at him.

Chapter 2

Consequences

"Have you lost your damn mind bringing this snake nigga into my club?" Freeway screamed at Jackal while still keeping the gun on Rozay.

"Freeway, it's not what you think," Rozay explained.

Rozay stood there frozen in place, not knowing what to do. He wasn't no punk, but he also knew Freeway would pull that trigger. There was a reason why Freeway was the boss in New Orleans. You couldn't be soft to run a city like the Big Easy. That was why he only wanted to talk about the deal with Jackal. But that wasn't going to happen. It really was Freeway's empire. Jackal was just his hitta.

"Listen, Freeway, let's talk about this like gentlemen."

"So, do you take me for a fool?"

"That's not what I'm trying to do here."

"Then tell me why the fuck you are here."

"It's just like what Jackal said. I'm trying to buy your empire."

"You got your own business, so why would you want mines?" Freeway still didn't put his gun away.

"Freeway, I'd feel more comfortable if you'd let me sit down and put that gun away."

"Come on, Freeway, put the gun away," Jackal pleaded.

"Why should I do that? Me and this nigga been beefing for over ten years. Now, he suddenly wants to buy my empire?" Freeway didn't trust anything that was about Rozay.

"I know we had beef, but it's not about that. I promise you. Just hear me out."

"You got five minutes of my time, so make it quick." Freeway sat down, but he didn't put the gun away. Instead, he just set it on the table.

"Can I please get a drink?" Freeway's actions rattled Rozay's nerves.

"Get your drink, and you're wasting time."

Rozay poured himself a drink, and his hands were shaking a little. He didn't know what was on Freeway's mind. Everybody knew how danger-ous Freeway could be. He only had a soft spot for Belladonna and showed her love. Rozay knew he had to tread carefully having this conversation.

"Now that you have your drink, tell me why after all these years, you want to end our rivalry and buy my empire." Freeway felt Rozay was up to no good.

"Honestly, we all know you'll get out of the game soon."

"Who the fuck told you that?"

"You been with Belladonna for ten years. I know you're going to marry her soon. Besides, you don't want no nigga trying you and using her as your weakness.""Have you lost your mind speaking about my girl? Her name shouldn't even be coming through your lips."

"I know how you feel about Belladonna, but what I speak of is the truth, and you know it." Rozay knew he was stepping into dangerous territory talking about Belladonna, but his point had to be made.

"Didn't I just tell you to watch your fucking mouth?" Freeway reached for his 9 mm.

Rozay was starting to get uncomfortable again now that Freeway had grabbed his gun. This was the only way he could convince Freeway to sell his empire to him. He was trying to persuade Freeway that as long as he ran his empire, Belladonna would not be safe. Jackal knew he would have to step in at any moment now. He saw the rage in Freeway's eyes hearing the word "Belladonna" come out of Rozay's mouth.

"I know you don't want to hear this, but Belladonna is your weakness."

"That's it. I've heard enough." He jumped up, flipped over the table, and smacked Rozay on the face with his pistol.

"Freeway, what the fuck, man?" Jackal tried to stop Freeway from his actions, but it was too late.

"Get your hands off me before I shoot your ass for setting up this fucked-up meeting." Now, Freeway pointed the gun in his partner's face.

"You *really* going to put a gun in my face?" Jackal was shocked.

Freeway ordered that Rozay be dragged out of his club. He had heard enough. He felt disrespected that this man was let into his club in the first place. Jackal had seen and heard enough from his partner. He also was about to leave . . . until Freeway stepped in front of him.

"Where the fuck do you think you're going?"

"First of all, Freeway, you need to get that gun out of my face. I'm your partner—*not* your enemy."

"*Are* you my partner? Any good partner wouldn't set up a meeting with a nigga I'm beefing with."

"I was trying to give you a way out. You're not the only one qualified to be a boss, you know."

Freeway took a step back after hearing the words that had just left his partner's deceiving lips. He had figured out what would happen if he had made the deal. Jackal would become partners with Rozay if Freeway sold his empire to him.

"You disloyal, ungrateful son of a bitch."

"What?"

"Don't you 'what' me, Jackal. You had planned on switching sides, didn't you?"

"It's not 'switching sides' if you're no longer in the game, Freeway."

"If we partners, we retire together. So you don't go off and start building a whole new empire with *my* connect."

"Freeway, do you know how selfish you sound?"

"Jackal, you better get out of my face before I put a bullet in your head."

Jackal just shook his head and walked off. Freeway's actions surprised him. But by the look in Freeway's eyes, he was not playing. This was why Jackal was trying to get Freeway out of the game. Once you mentioned Belladonna, he would lose it. This behavior could cost Freeway everything. Freeway didn't understand Jackal's logic in all this. He only looked at it as Jackal replacing him as the boss of New Orleans. Freeway looked at his custom-made Rolex and realized it was past midnight. It was time for him to see if Belladonna had made it home yet.

Freeway walked past the club guards and let them know he was headed home and to let the girls back in the VIP section. Then he walked outside, feeling the crisp air running across his face. As he started his car, he thought about the night he had just had. He was tired of the headaches he was getting from running his business. Maybe he should retire, he thought. He drove about twenty minutes until he pulled up in his driveway.

Freeway hit his remote to open his garage door. When he saw that Belladonna's car was not in the garage, he instantly grew furious. He didn't even pull his Range Rover into the garage. Instead, he just parked his car, jumped out, and ran inside the mansion to see if she was inside. He checked every single room, but she was nowhere in sight. Then he pulled out his phone and called her, but the call went to voicemail all three times he called.

He walked in circles around his living room, wondering where in the hell she could be. He wondered how she could be this reckless. He walked over to the bar and poured himself a shot. Quickly gulping down the first drink, he poured another. He tried to call her again, but it still went to voicemail. Finally, he had no choice but to drive to Rozay's club. He put a full clip in his gun when he got to his car. He was prepared to shoot anybody he had to over the whereabouts of Belladonna.

He jumped into his Range Rover again and headed to where he didn't want Belladonna to go in the first place. So many things ran through his mind—and none were good. He knew for a fact that Belladonna had never turned off her phone. That was a rule that they both lived by just in case something bad happened—and this was bad. He pulled up to the curb in front of Rozay's club and jumped out with his gun in hand.

Since Freeway was well known, people became afraid when he showed up at the front door with his gun. The bouncer saw him approaching and didn't know what to do. Freeway was nobody to play with. He would shoot you just as quickly as you called your own name. The bouncer tried talking calmly to Freeway, but he wasn't having it.

"Come on, Freeway, you know you can't come up here like this with that firearm." The bouncer was nervous.

"If I were you, fatso, I'd move." Freeway cocked his gun and pointed it right at the bouncer's head.

"Please, Freeway, this is not necessary."

"When it comes to my Belladonna, this is *very* necessary. Now, I'm going to ask you one more time—move."

"If that's what you want, I can have her pulled out of the club."

"What the fuck you waiting on? Make the call."

The bouncer wasted no time. He got on his walkie-talkie and called the inside to find Freeway's girl and bring her outside. Ten minutes passed, and there was no callback to the bouncer's walkie-talkie. Finally, he saw that Freeway was getting agitated, so he made the call again. Impatient, Freeway hit the bouncer in the head and made his way inside the club.

It was like when Freeway walked through the door, things started moving in slow motion. People knew it was not good that the infamous man was in this club. But he didn't have to worry about moving through a crowd. People automatically got out of his way. The first spot Freeway hit was the DJ's booth. He walked up the small steps and put the gun to the DJ's head.

"Do you know who I am?"

"Of course I do, Freeway." The DJ started pissing on himself out of fear.

"You know Belladonna, right?"

"Yes, Freeway," muttered the DJ.

"I'm going to ask you this one time. Have you seen her tonight?" Freeway put pressure on the gun he held against the DJ's temple.

"I saw her with Asia earlier on the dance floor."

"Where is she now?"

"Honestly, I don't know. I lost sight of them once I started spinning and hyping up the club."

"You know what I will do to you if you lie to me, right?"

"Come on, Freeway, I'm just the DJ. I wouldn't lie to you about this. We all know what Belladonna means to you."

Freeway decided to let the DJ go. He could tell by his amount of fear that he had no intention of lying to him. When he walked back down the steps, Freeway was met by Rozay's head of security. He noticed the man was holding a .45. Freeway laughed as he saw fear in his eyes.

"What the fuck you going to do with that? You don't have the fucking balls to aim your gun at me, boy?"

"Freeway, please. Rozay wants to speak with you in his office. Let these people go back to the party."

"Your boss better have some answers for me."

Freeway made his way off the dance floor and went to the back of the club where Rozay's office was. When he walked into the office, he saw Asia sitting at a long table with Rozay wearing a stoic look on her face. Freeway immediately raised his gun, pointing it at both of them.

"What the fuck happened?"

"I think you better sit down, Freeway," Rozay suggested while holding a bag of ice on his face due to the pistol-whipping he took from Freeway earlier.

"I'm not sitting nowhere. One of you better start talking, and I do mean now."

"Look, Freeway, we will all feel a little better if you would sit down and put the gun down. Damn, look what you did to my fucking face earlier."

"So what? You got balls now because you sitting in your own club? I don't give a fuck about these people. I'll shoot everybody in this damn room."

"Belladonna was kidnapped!" Asia blurted out.

Chapter 3

Proposal

Freeway damn near dropped his gun when he heard that his lady was kidnapped. He got weak in his knees. His worst nightmare had come true. He was afraid of this, but who had the balls to kidnap his woman? Damn near everybody in the city feared him, but who was the 1 percent that didn't? It had to be a visitor to the city, he thought. Then without thinking, he pulled out a chair and sat down.

"I was on my to your house to tell you, Freeway. But I know you don't fuck with me or Rozay."

"Wait a fucking minute." Freeway snapped out of his daze and raised his gun again.

"What?" Asia jumped back.

"How the fuck did my Belladonna get kidnapped, but you didn't?"

"We were out back smoking a blunt. Then a blue van pulled up, snatched her up, and someone put a gun in my face. He handed me a note with a number to give to you." Asia handed Freeway the small, folded piece of paper.

"Freeway, I told you this was going to happen," Rozay reminded him.

"Nigga, don't make me shoot you." Freeway snatched the note out of Asia's hand and left the room.

He walked back through the dance floor, out of the building, and waited until he got in his car to make the call. Once inside the vehicle, he rolled up the window. He didn't want anyone to know Belladonna had been taken and somebody was trying his hand. Then he made the call.

"Hello." He could tell this person was using a voice app that disguised their voice, making it sound robotic and deep.

"What the fuck gives you the right to snatch my girl?"

"Shut up, bitch-ass nigga."

"What, motherfucker? You know who you talking to?" Freeway screamed into the phone.

"I know *exactly* who I'm talking to—a man that cares about his money and nothing else."

"Everybody in the streets knows that Belladonna is my heart."

"Is she? I think otherwise.

Well, now, Freeway has something to prove. Let's see if you love your fiancée-to-be or your precious empire."

"If you hurt Belladonna, I will find and kill you."

"That's funny you say that because I injected poison into her body. In forty-eight hours, it will kill her. So you have two choices as I see it."

"What the hell is that?" For the first time, Freeway felt helpless.

"You either let her live and give up your whole empire to save this woman—point-blank period . . . or else. But to be fair, you have three hours to think about it before I inject this poison in her."

"I thought you already did it."

"No, I was just playing with you, but I will." The mysterious person let off a devilish laugh.

"You think this a fucking game to play with me like this?"

"You have struck fear in people's hearts for over ten years. You about to know what it feels like to drop to your knees and beg for mercy for once in your life." The mysterious voice hung up.

After hearing the phone go dead, Freeway damn near lost his mind. How could he let this happen? He had to figure out how to save Belladonna *and* keep his empire. He worked too hard to hand his empire over to somebody like this. This had to be somebody that knew who he was. He looked at his watch and realized Rozay was probably home, so he headed to his house.

Freeway wasted no time getting to his destination. He saw several cars parked at Rozay's house, but at this point, he didn't care. He got out of his car, popped the trunk, removed the red carpet, and pulled out his M16. He wanted answers, and dammit, he was going to get them. He found it funny Belladonna was kidnapped but not Asia. This didn't sit right with him. Even if someone had to lose their life tonight, he would find Belladonna. He put a full round clip in his M16 and headed to the front door. Freeway had no intention of knocking. He kicked the door in and shot in the air.

"Everybody get the fuck down!"

"What the fuck, Freeway? Are you crazy?" Rozay jumped up from the poker table he was sitting.

"No, I'm not crazy, but you better come clean about Belladonna's kidnapping."

Freeway walked over and grabbed Asia by her hair and threw her to the ground. Then he stuck his assault rifle to the back of her head. She started crying and screaming for Rozay's assistance. This was funny to Freeway since Asia and Rozay claimed they didn't like each other. Rozay ran over but stopped in his tracks when Freeway shot in the air again.

"I thought you didn't like Asia. You better tell me something before I shoot this bitch." Now, Freeway stepped on the middle of her back."OK, OK, we act this way so nobody will use her against me."

"You better tell me the truth about Belladonna's kidnapping."

"Honestly, we gave you the information we had."

"It's a coincidence you came to my club saying somebody would use Belladonna as my weakness, and tonight, she comes up kidnapped."

"Freeway, stop this!"

Freeway was shocked when he turned around and saw his partner, Jackal. He lifted his foot off Asia's back and turned his full attention to his partner. Jackal had a huge grin on his face. Freeway found nothing funny and wondered why his partner was at Rozay's house in the first place.

"Jackal, why the hell are you here?"

"That would be the question of the day. First, we need to step outside."

"Me and you have nothing to talk about."

"Oh, but I think we do, that is, if you want Belladonna back."

"You know where she is?"

"As I said, we need to step outside."

Freeway walked outside, following behind Jackal. Jackal had no fear in his heart. He knew he had the upper hand at the moment. Jackal pulled out his phone and made a call. After waiting for somebody to answer, he told the person to get her on the phone, then handed Freeway the phone.

"Freeway, please, help me!" Belladonna screamed into the phone.

"Baby, please, hold on!" Freeway responded.

Jackal jerked the phone out of Freeway's hand. Freeway couldn't believe his partner of ten years was behind the kidnapping. Jackal had that wicked grin on his face again. He put the phone back into his pocket.

"How could you? We were partners."

"We weren't partners. You was always the boss, right?"

"If you had a problem, you should have said something."

"Nigga, I tried to give you a way out, but you turned down the deal."

Freeway realized that Jackal must have been planning on turning his back on him for years. He just was waiting on the right time to do so. Jackal pulled out a cigar and lit it. Freeway hated the fact that Jackal felt so relaxed.

"So, what do I have to do to get Belladonna back?" Freeway had to humble himself.

"Don't ask stupid questions. You know exactly what I want."

"How much will it cost me?"

"I want your whole empire."

"Have you lost your mind, Jackal?"

"No. But I think you lost yours, doubting me all these years like you were really better than me. Belladonna was the one thing that made you weak in these streets."

For the first time, he did feel weak and exposed. He knew he had no choice but to give up his empire. This was the only way to get back Belladonna. He was sick and tired of her being away from him. If he had to give up his empire, then it had to happen.

"I tell you what. I'll be nice. If you just give me fifty mil and your contacts—of course, you must retire—then I'll give you Belladonna—*only* because we have history."

"Fine."

Jackal stuck out his hand to shake Freeway's. No matter how much he didn't want to, he did anyway. For the first time, Freeway wasn't in control or the boss anymore. Jackal had been scheming to be on top for years. He never wanted to bring Belladonna into his game plan, but there was no other way to beat Freeway, so he did it. Jackal walked off, heading back into Rozay's house . . . until he heard his name being called.

"I never thought that you would stoop this low or be the one to turn on me."

"It's like you once said. It's always the ones that are close to you."

"Yeah, maybe you're right, but why are you in Rozay's house?"

"There's a guy at the poker table that has to be dealt with. Meet me at your club at three a.m. so we can make the exchange."

"OK." Freeway got into his car and drove off.

When he got home, his mind made him feel like a failure. He was upstairs throwing all the money out of his safe onto the bed, money he had worked hard for. He stuffed it into two duffle bags. When he zipped up the last duffle bag, he reminded himself that Belladonna was worth every penny.

It seemed like time was on a fast track because it was now a quarter to three. He decided to head to his club because it would be time for the exchange by the time he got there.

He walked into his club and turned on all the lights. Then he threw the money bags on the pool table and went behind the bar to make himself a stiff drink. He definitely needed it. He turned the drink up as if it were water.

Suddenly, someone knocked hard on the front door of the club. He already knew who it was. He unlocked the door to let in Jackal. Freeway grew angry when he didn't see Belladonna with Jackal.

"Are you playing with me right now?"

"I'm no fool, Freeway. I need to see the money first."

"Whatever, nigga." Freeway walked over to the pool table, unzipped the bags, and dumped out all the money.

Once Jackal saw all the money, he called for Belladonna to be escorted inside the club. When Freeway saw her, he ran over to her, and they kissed like they had been apart for years. Freeway made her go into his office, but she grabbed his hand instead.

"Freeway, please, let it go."

"Baby, go in the back. It's not what you think."

Jackal was about to grab his gun. He still knew that Freeway was a very dangerous man, and he was not for one second going to underestimate him one bit—not now—not ever.

"I have to admit you got the best of me." Freeway put his hand out to shake Jackal's hand.

"This was only business, Freeway." They shook hands.

"I'm no dummy. You didn't come up with this plan alone. You *do* know one day I'll be a boss again. So enjoy it now and get out of my club."

Jackal left the club knowing he was leaving a very dangerous, vengeful man living.

Chapter 4

Deeper than the Game

Belladonna was sitting in the back, thinking she was about to hear gunfire, but she didn't. She honestly never thought Jackal had the balls to do what he did. However, Freeway showed her that he loved her more than his empire. She jumped a little when Freeway came walking through the office door.

"So, does this answer your question, boo?" Freeway asked with a smile.

"Yes, it does. I just wish it didn't have to be answered this way. But, Freeway, I never wanted you to lose any of your empire." Belladonna felt bad.

"Belladonna, this is deeper than love. This is the bond that we share. I would have given it all up for you, but you were right about one thing."

"What was that?"

"Jackal turned out to be a rotten apple." Freeway banged his fist on the table.

"Baby, I'm sorry I was right. I really am."

"I'm just pissed he used you to do it, that's all."

Belladonna leaned over and kissed Freeway on the lips very softly. He had forgotten how soft her lips were. Then without thinking, he slid his tongue inside her mouth, pulled off her blouse, and took her whole breast into his mouth.

She unzipped his pants, moaning about how much she missed his dick. When she pulled it out, it was already standing at attention. She knelt, taking all ten inches into her mouth, her saliva slithering down his balls. Her long tongue wrapped around his dick, causing his eyes to roll back in his head, making him look at the ceiling. He grabbed a handful of her hair and fucked her mouth ever so gently.

Then Belladonna jumped on the table, pulling off her pants and panties. Freeway wasted no time. He thrust his dick deep inside her. She wrapped her legs around him, feeling the love with every stroke he gave her. All the pain he felt while she was gone went into his strokes.

"I love you, Belladonna," he yelled as he exploded inside her. They both climaxed at the same time. It seemed like their love grew during their separation. Then Belladonna put on her clothes but couldn't help feeling bad about her man's loss. Freeway went to the bar and pulled out a wine bottle and two tall tube glasses. Belladonna smiled.

"What's the celebration?" she asked, picking up her glass.

"To freedom." Freeway picked up his glass and lightly touched hers.

Belladonna thought that this was what she wanted, to have her man all to herself. To have all his love devoted to her and not the streets. But what was the point if he was not fully happy? She felt like she was being selfish. Freeway worked so hard to have New Orleans on lock, and she thought it was her fault so much of it was taken away from him.

"You don't have to pretend, Freeway."

"Belladonna, what are you talking about?"

There is no way Belladonna is still unhappy, Freeway thought.

"Giving up so much of your empire. I know it wasn't cheap getting me back."

"It's fine, Belladonna. It really is."

"Freeway, stop fucking lying to me." Finally, Belladonna stood up out of anger and frustration.

"Why are you getting upset? We're back together, so calm down." Freeway went to grab her hand, but she snatched it away.

"Your empire meant the world to you, and you worked hard to be the boss. No matter how much I wanted you out of the streets, it was not fair to you to have half your empire snatched away by a motherfucker who didn't work for it." Belladonna's blood was boiling.

"Baby, it's fine. Please, calm down."

"Freeway, I don't understand. Much of your empire is gone, and you're not mad. If you truly love me, show me how you feel right now."

"I did what I had to do to get you back. Am I mad that my so-called partner turned out to be a snake? You damn right I am. However, that's part of the game. The streets will use what you love the most against you."

"Freeway, I'm going to ask you a question, and I don't care how much love you have for me. I want the truth."

"OK, I'm listening."

"Do you want your empire and position back?"

"Belladonna, you know I do, but I made a deal to retire when I got you back." Freeway dropped his head in defeat.

"We're going to get your empire back together as a couple and on one condition."

"What's that?"

"That we get married tonight."

"You know I have no problem with that, bae. You're my lady."

"There is one other thing. Not only will you be my husband, but *I'm* also your new partner in getting your money back. We'll make Jackal think you're out of the game for good. After we get married, you contact him and convince him, so his guard will be down."

"Damn, baby, when did you become so street savvy? You turning me the fuck on."

"By watching my husband-to-be all these years, now, let's go."

Freeway didn't know what got into Belladonna, but he damn sure was loving every bit of it. They went to the chapel and had a little ceremony to become husband and wife. Being together for over ten years, they already felt married anyway. But instead of a honeymoon, they were working on a plan to take back Freeway's empire, but now, as a dominant power couple. Freeway was about to call Jackal but hung up and looked over at his wife.

"Before we do this, let me take you out, baby, and discuss our new future. Let your man wine and dine you. This other shit can wait. We were just separated, so let me enjoy you."

"You know what? I think you're right." Belladonna licked her lips. Her man was looking like a whole snack right now.

They eventually settled in at the Restaurant Bones. Freeway loved the steak and potatoes, and carrots there. A bottle of red wine sat on the table. Freeway admired Belladonna's beauty from across the table. The light of the room had her beauty blowing. She took a sip of her water. "To us." Freeway raised his glass.

"To new beginnings," Belladonna toasted with her husband.

"So, Belladonna, you know I got to ask . . ." Freeway was curious.

"What's that, my love?"

"Why the change of heart?"

"What do you mean?" Belladonna began to cut her steak.

"You know what I mean. All these years, you complained about me being in the streets. Why the change of heart?"

"My feelings for the streets have not changed. I still think they're grimy and cutthroat. We both know the street loves nobody but itself. However, I refuse to sit back. So, I'd rather us do this as a couple than you do it alone. But when you get your empire back, we done."

"Fair enough, babe." Freeway wiped his wife's mouth with his napkin, then kissed her on the forehead.

"Go ahead and make that call." Belladonna smiled while taking a sip of her wine.

"I have a question for you."

"What's that?"

"You not scared?"

"Why should I be? I'm married to one of the most ruthless bosses in New Orleans. Now, stop stalling and make the call."

His lady had spoken. He took his phone out to call Jackal. However, just as he was doing so, he spotted Jackal at the front counter making a pickup order. He thought to himself it couldn't get any better than this. This was his chance to do what he had to do in person. He and Belladonna looked at each other. Then she told him to go handle his business. He swallowed his wine, threw his napkin on the table, and approached Jackal.

"We need to talk," Freeway said while tapping Jackal on the shoulder.

"Damn, what's up, Freeway?" Jackal was shaken a little seeing Freeway.

"Look, man, now that I got Belladonna back, I don't care about nothing else. So, here's the name of my connect." Freeway asked the lady behind the counter for some paper and a pen. Then he wrote down the connect he used to buy his drugs.

"You really not going to come after me?"

"I almost lost my woman to these streets. I'm done." He handed Jackal the piece of paper with the information.

"So, we cool?" Jackal asked nervously.

"We may never talk again, but on a street beef, yeah, we cool." He gave Jackal some dap, and Jackal walked off. Freeway noticed he had dropped his receipt. He picked it up, walked over to his table, and handed it to Belladonna.

"What's this?" She grabbed the receipt.

"Just read it," he suggested.

"It says, 'Rozay.'"

"Exactly. Why would Jackal be picking up food for Rozay?"

"They're working together." Belladonna got mad and balled up the receipt.

"Just as I suspected. They both planned your kidnapping. You know damn well Asia had to be in on it too."

"Don't worry. I'll pay that bitch a visit at her hair salon first thing in the morning." Belladonna called for the check from the waitress.

After a long, sumptuous meal, they returned home to settle in. Freeway called his connect and told him to give Jackal anything he asked for. He wanted everything to go as planned. Then he got off the phone and lay beside his woman, wrapping his arms around her. She felt so warm and safe in his arms. She was determined to make everybody pay that double-crossed them. She realized that Asia had been playing her this whole time.

"Whatever happens, Freeway, you better not let me die in these streets at the hands of these fools. I'm giving you the green light to be as ruthless as I know you can be."

"Baby, I'll never hold back when it comes to you. We Bonnie and Clyde, except this ending will be different." Freeway wouldn't let any harm come to Belladonna, even if he had to put his life on the line.

"What are you planning on doing to Asia?"

Carl Weber's Kingpins: New Orleans   49

"That bitch is about to come up missing."

"That's my girl." Freeway smiled and kept on holding his woman until they fell asleep in that exact position.

Belladonna got up the following day, took a shower, and threw her hair in a ponytail. She put on a grey jogging suit and some Puma sneakers. They got in the car, drove to Asia Hair Salon, and parked across the street. Freeway could tell that Belladonna already had a plan in motion.

"How you planning on getting her, boo?"

"This bitch is so predictable. She goes to Waffle House every day for lunch." Belladonna had an evil grin on her face.

From how she acted, Freeway realized his wife had the street life in her the whole time. She just refused to act on it. Finally, after waiting another thirty minutes, they spotted Asia walking down the street like life was peachy. Sure enough, she was heading straight for the Waffle House. Little did she know today, she would not get a chance to taste scrambled eggs with cheese and bacon.

They drove the car up to her as soon as she turned the corner. Freeway hit the trunk button as Belladonna jumped out.

"Did you think you would be safe in these streets, bitch?" Belladonna pulled out her gun, hit Asia on the back of the head, and dragged her to the trunk of her car.

Asia was crying, asking for forgiveness. But Belladonna's mind was set on redemption for her and her husband. So she told Asia it was pay-up time . . . and shut the trunk.

Chapter 5

Love & Redemption

Belladonna and Freeway pulled up to the house, but her husband grabbed her arm before Belladonna could get out of the car. He had some concerns. Belladonna was ready to pull Asia out of the trunk. Freeway had so much love for Belladonna that he didn't want her to do something that she might regret later in life. He knew the pain the street life could cost someone.

"Hold on, Belladonna."

"What?"

"Are you sure about this?"

"What do you mean? Don't tell me that you're having second thoughts."

"I never said that. I just don't want you to do something that you may regret later."

"Freeway, these people tried to destroy our lives. This is about our love and redemption."

"Once we pull this bitch out of the trunk, there's no turning back, Belladonna. You *do* realize that, right?"

"I wouldn't dream of it. Now, let's go, but first, kiss me."

Freeway grabbed her chin and kissed her seductively. Then they got out of the car. Freeway entered the house while Belladonna went to the trunk to confront Asia. When she opened the trunk, Asia was balled up, crying. Belladonna could tell Asia was not built for the mess she caused herself, but she felt no shame or pity for her ex-friend.

Belladonna ordered her to get out of the car, grabbed a handful of her hair, and pulled her out. She kicked her in the stomach, causing her to fall, then made her get off the ground and walk into the house. They took a sharp right as soon as they walked through the door and went down to the basement. It was dark. The darkness alone scared Asia. Belladonna kicked her in the back, knocking her down the steps and making her hit the cold basement floor.

Freeway had three thick sheets of plastic laid out on the floor. Belladonna grabbed Asia by the wrist and dragged her on the plastic. Asia started shaking when she felt the friction of the plastic. She knew seeing plastic in a basement could not be good at all. Belladonna said nothing for two whole minutes. She just walked in circles and looked at Asia with anger burning in her eyes.

"Be honest with me. Were you *ever* my damn friend?"

"Yes," Asia spoke through her tears.

"Bitch, don't lie to me." Belladonna kicked her in the stomach. "Belladonna, I swear I was . . . at first."

"What changed?"

"Your man is what changed. People got tired of him being the boss."

"Who, Rozay?"

"My husband." Asia was almost afraid to give the answer she just spat out.

"Your husband? Wait, you don't have a husband."

"Yes, I do. Rozay is really my husband, and Jackal is my kinfolk." Asia just spilled the truth that never should have been told.

"Why did you two lie like this?"

"Because Rozay didn't want the streets to use me as his weakness like we did with you and Freeway. You were the key to bringing down the boss of New Orleans."

"You know Freeway will snap when I tell him this, right?"

"Please, Belladonna, I just want to live. I never wanted to get involved."

"Well, you did your share of becoming trash. You sit tight. I'll be right back."

Belladonna walked upstairs and saw her husband sitting in their all-white living room, watching their sixty-four-inch smart TV. She was amazed at how calm he could be through street activity. She went to the bar, poured a drink for them, and then handed him one while kissing him on the cheek. She told him everything Asia had just revealed to her. Freeway just shook his head at all the lies.

"You know, I should feel honored," he laughed.

"Why? All of them are full of lies and bullshit."

"They had to lie and kidnap you just to defeat me, fucking losers."

"Do you think I should kill her?"

"Belladonna, I will not let you kill anybody. Your hands must stay clean, but she has to stay hidden until I handle Jackal and Rozay. If she dies, *I* will be the one to end her life. Just you riding with me as my wife is all I could ask for."

"Freeway, look at me."

"Yeah, bae?" He cut off the TV.

"I want you to know that you're my everything, and I will pull that trigger for you." A tear rolled down her face.

"Baby, I don't want to give you that power. Pulling that trigger might ignite a fire inside you that can't be put out." He wiped away her tears.

"I just want to be your backbone."

"I know, boo."

"It's my fault you lost half your money in the first place."

"Stop blaming yourself for a fool's actions. I will reign supreme when all this is done."

"*We* will reign supreme. We're a team, remember?" Belladonna smiled at her husband.

Freeway cocked his gun, got off the couch, and headed for the basement. He told his wife to follow him. She finished her drink to kill her nerves. Freeway told her to pour another drink, then meet him in the basement. Belladonna did just that. When Asia saw the infamous Freeway approach her as she lay on the floor, she began to piss on herself. She knew the danger that his presence brought.

"I'm going to ask you one time. Where the fuck is my money?"

"Don't make him ask you twice." Belladonna walked up, handing Freeway the drink.

"You the one that's going to need that." He gave her the pistol.

"OK." She gulped down the drink while taking the weapon.

Asia saw her life flash before her eyes as the gun switched from Freeway's hand to Belladonna's. Asia waited no time, telling Freeway that his money was hidden in her husband's barbershop behind a picture of Rozay's parents. Freeway smiled at the fact that Asia was disloyal to her husband. He knew for a fact Belladonna loved him and would never snitch.

"Kill this bitch." Freeway took a step back and stood behind his wife.

Belladonna stepped up and looked at her ex-friend. Her hand began to shake, not because she was in fear but because of anger. All the shit Asia caused started flashing through her mind. The fact that they stole her husband's money became a major motivation. Before she knew it, she ran up and grabbed Asia by her hair.

"This is for the pain you cost my husband, bitch. *He's* the real King of New Orleans—not *your* husband." Then Belladonna shot Asia twice in the head.

Freeway was shocked. He just knew Belladonna would hand him the gun and say she couldn't do it. There was no turning back now. He was so turned on by what she just did. She handed him the gun and told him to meet her immediately in the bedroom.

Freeway rolled up Asia's corpse in the plastic, stapling the ends together. Then he ran upstairs to see what his wife needed. He just knew he would find her on the edge of the bed in tears, but he was in for a shock.

When he got upstairs, she was naked and demanded he pull out his dick. Killing Asia had her sex drive shooting through the roof. She was so horny. Freeway wasn't moving fast enough. She unzipped his pants and started sucking his dick. Freeway was losing his mind. It felt so good.

Belladonna sucked on his dick, then wrapped her tongue under his balls, making him weak in his knees.

"Fuck—you must want me to beat that pussy up." Freeway picked her up and put her on the dresser as he spread her legs.

"Baby, please, take this pussy. It's craving you."

Freeway ran his fingers across her pussy lips. She was so creamy and wet. Then he grabbed her by the throat and forced his dick inside her. She yelled out. Freeway was fucking her as hard as he could. Like this was their last sex session ever. She was creaming all over his dick. He began to suck on her nipples. Her breasts were so sensitive, and it had her gushing out her sweet juices.

"Whose pussy is this?"

"It's yours, baby. Fuck me like a dirty bitch, please . . ."

He bent her over and stuck his dick in her ass. She spread her ass cheeks and took all his dick inside her. Being fucked hard in the ass brought up flashes of killing Asia. She kept saying, "harder, harder." Before you knew it, Freeway had come all in her ass. All his energy went into giving her the best sex session ever. Finally, he collapsed on her back. Belladonna was amazed that her killing somebody would give her the best sex session ever.

She gathered the rest of her energy and walked into the bathroom to shower. Freeway fell back on the bed. The room was spinning.

He had to hurry up and get her out of the street life. He could tell that her spirit and energy were starting to turn dark. He had to save the little bit of innocence she had left.

When the cold water hit Belladonna's body, it felt like her pain was hitting the tub and going down the drain. The bad part was that she didn't feel any remorse for killing Asia.

Freeway knocked on the bathroom door and interrupted her thoughts.

"Yeah, baby, I'm almost done," she yelled from the shower.

"I'm going to get rid of this body."

"You want me to come with you?" She was about to step out of the shower.

"No, boo, it's easier if it's just me."

Freeway didn't want her to see Asia's body getting chopped up and fed to pigs. She definitely wasn't ready for that part of the life he lived.

After Freeway left, Belladonna stepped out of the shower and dried off. She grabbed her robe and walked to the basement. She was amazed at how her husband cleaned the floor. No blood was there. She was in awe. Her husband was certainly a professional. She definitely knew that this was *not* his first rodeo. She was in a daze thinking of

how many people her husband had killed in his
years on the streets. Now, she knew why he was
infamous and was the boss and why people wanted
him knocked off the top. It was because he was
feared.

She realized he only was protecting her innocence. That's why he never wanted her to ride with
him or attend business meetings at his club. She
ran upstairs and sat on the couch when she heard
him returning.

"Damn, you got rid of that quick."

"You know, I know people." He smiled.

"Freeway, we need to talk."

"That's funny. I was going to say the same thing
to you."

"I want to help you get this money back, but I
don't want this life to continue after you do."

"I understand your concern, and once we lock
down New Orleans, I will make sure nobody will
dare test my power in the streets again."

"You're going to make an example out of Jackal
and Rozay, aren't you?"

"No. *We* are."

They left, returned to their city home, turned
on Netflix, and fell asleep on the couch with
Belladonna snuggling under his arms. No matter
the dirt she did, she felt safe with Freeway.

Chapter 6

Love Conquers All

When Belladonna woke up, she noticed her husband was not on the couch. On a typical day, she would lie back down, but with everything going on, she decided to check the house. When she got up, she smelled the aroma of eggs and bacon in the air, so she headed for the kitchen. Freeway had fixed her a full breakfast of waffles, eggs, bacon, and fried ham with a side of orange juice. He even had a rose in a vase sitting in the middle of the table.

"What's all this?" she asked while stretching.

"What? A man can't cook for his wife?" He pulled out a chair for her to sit down.

"I'm not saying that. I just thought you'd be in a hurry to handle business."

"One thing you need to learn, baby girl. Those that rush, rush into trouble."

"Yeah, I guess you got a point. You're the expert."
Belladonna giggled a little.

When Freeway was about to join her at the table,
his doorbell rang. They both looked at each other.
Freeway told her to stay put, that he would handle
it. He went to the door and opened it. There stood
Rozay in tears. Freeway had a pretty good idea
why he was at his house. However, Freeway felt no
remorse for Rozay with his double-crossing ways.

Freeway reached into the pocket of his robe and
pulled out a cigar and a lighter. He lit it up before
asking the question to which he already knew the
answer.

"Nigga, is there a reason why you disturbing me
and my wife? After just cooking her a nice breakfast, I'd like to sit with her and enjoy our morning."

"You got to help me."

"Me help you? Nigga, you got the audacity even
to fix your lips to say that."

"Asia is missing."

"Why should I give a fuck?"

"Come on, man. You just went through the same
shit." His tears were cascading down his face now.

"You do realize I know you were part of the plan
of kidnapping my wife?"

Rozay's eyes widened. He had no idea that
Freeway knew. He was more surprised Freeway
had not shot him yet. He began to back up slowly.
Actually, he was ready to take off running. Freeway

blew a thick cloud of smoke in his direction out of disrespect for the man standing before him.

"I also know you lied about Asia being your enemy. You stand in my fucking doorway crying like a bitch, and you didn't even love her enough to claim her as your wife. All because you were scared the streets would snatch her up. News flash, nigga, you are weak." Freeway blew another thick cloud in his face.

"You don't understand, Freeway. Nobody could defeat you."

"So, that gives you the right to kidnap my fiancée, fool?"

"Now, mines is missing, and people fear you. I'll pay you."

Freeway thought it was ironic that he would offer to pay him, knowing it was his money in the first place. He laughed at the suggestion Rozay had just made and slammed the door in his face. Then he went back to the kitchen and sat down with Belladonna.

"Was that Rozay?"

"Yeah."

"Why did you miss the opportunity to end him?"

"He'll be last on our list. He's already ready to crack over Asia being missing."

"You know it's amazing."

"What's that?" Freeway made him something to eat.

"These dudes act so tough, like they're built for the life . . . until some real shit happens to them."

"That's all the time. Now, finish up. We're going to the beach today."

"Hold up. The beach?" She stopped Freeway in his tracks before he ran upstairs.

"Yeah, I want to treat my wife to a day of relaxation."

"I understand all that, but shouldn't you hurry up and get this situation over with?"

"Belladonna, this situation is like a delicate flower, so let me handle it as I see fit. Now, go get dressed for the beach."

Despite how Belladonna felt, she knew her man had been running things in the streets for over twenty years, so she trusted his decision. She just wanted things to go back to normal. She quickly grabbed her bikini, threw on some clothes, and then headed out to the beach with her husband. Regardless, she was going to enjoy the day with Freeway. Besides, she knew Rozay and Jackal were losing their minds, not knowing what Freeway was thinking.

When they reached the beach, Belladonna had changed into her $200 bathing suit. She laid a towel out on the sand and soaked in the sun. Freeway was out in the water. She admired her man's muscular body from afar. She had one ruthless, sexy man, she thought. No matter how this situation played out, she knew Freeway would protect her and take a bullet for her if he had to.

Minutes later, Freeway came out of the water to check on her.

"You good, baby?" he saw the sorry look that her face was babysitting.

"Yeah, I just want this all to be over, you know."

"It will be. Just let me handle it the right way. Then we never have to deal with this again. Don't worry."

"I know you will, but I got to know something."

"Yeah? What is it?"

"Tell me the truth, Freeway." She wanted to know the truth and didn't want Freeway to worry about protecting her feelings.

"OK, but hurry up so we can get back to our day at the beach."

"Are you going to kill them?" Belladonna looked straight into Freeway's eyes.

"What they did was unforgivable. They put your life in jeopardy. They must pay the full price."

"I understand." She knew the answer to her question.

In all honesty, she couldn't blame him for how he felt. His own partner betrayed him and kidnapped her, so she knew he would not let this slide with a pass.

Chapter 7

King & Queen

Freeway pulled into the driveway of their home. They saw Jackal sitting on their front porch. Freeway couldn't stop the car fast enough before Belladonna grabbed the gun out of the console and jumped out of the car, running up to him. Jackal quickly stood up from his sitting position.

"Nigga, have you lost your damn mind sitting on my porch after the shit you caused?"

"Calm down. I just want to talk."

"I should put a bullet in your head right now."

"I'll handle this, baby. You go ahead in the house." Freeway was shocked at the rage Belladonna let loose. Belladonna handed the gun to her husband and rolled her eyes at Jackal as she walked into the house. Jackal jumped a little after hearing the door slam. Freeway tucked the gun away and stared at Jackal, waiting for him to explain why he was there.

"Look, Freeway, I'm not dumb. I know Asia is dead. Rozay may be dumb enough to keep looking for her, but I know you killed her. Hell, the way Belladonna just went off, *she* probably killed her."

"You got some nerve to come on my property and accuse me of murder."

"Come on, Freeway, we kidnapped the first lady of New Orleans, and now, Asia comes up missing. That's no coincidence. I know Asia will never be seen again. I had no business fucking with the first lady of New Orleans, but please, Freeway, let's end this peacefully." Jackal wanted a peaceful ending to all the mess he had started. Deep down, he knew neither he nor Rozay was any match for Freeway.

"There is no war, and I know nothing about Asia or where she is. I told you I no longer indulge in the life."

"These mind games you're playing don't fool me one bit." Jackal was getting angry, knowing Freeway was after them.

"You need to take that bass out of your voice when talking to me." Freeway smiled after his statement.

"So, this the game you're going to play?"

"By the way, I know Asia is your bitch. For ten years, you lied to me. We was never partners. Now, get the fuck off my property."

"Freeway, I can explain—" Jackal started to feel fear.

Freeway pulled out his gun and called for Belladonna to come outside. She immediately came out and stood on the porch. Freeway threw her the gun and started smiling, but his eyes were wild with rage.

"Now, I'm going to tell you one more time, get the fuck off my property before I give the order to end you."

"Since when does Belladonna shoot people?" Jackal never knew her to be a killer.

"Try me, bitch." She fired the gun, sending a bullet two inches from Jackal's right foot.

Jackal jumped back, falling to the ground. He couldn't believe that Belladonna had shot at him. *When did she become a street diva?* he thought. He considered returning Freeway's money. Maybe that would change things.

"Freeway, I could bring back your money as a peace offering, please."

"You keep that money you should never have taken in the first place. You'll have to live with the disloyalty you showed to my husband. Now, get away from my house." This time, Belladonna had the pistol aimed at Jackal's head.

Jackal scrambled to his feet and ran to his car, which was parked down the street. After Jackal realized they didn't want the money returned, he knew he and Rozay were in trouble. He created a mess that he knew Freeway wouldn't let go of. Freeway and Belladonna were bosses of New Orleans, and they were out to prove that.

Belladonna looked at her husband. She could tell by his expression that he was proud of her. She handed him the gun as he walked up and kissed her on the cheek, but there was something she didn't understand. She needed to know what her husband's game plan was.

"We could have ended him just now. So why did you let him escape?" Belladonna wondered.

"Because he was expecting it. Trust me; *we* are in control."

"Did I do right by not accepting the money back?" She wanted to make him proud.

"Of course you did. The game plan is to give them the illusion we're not after them. Their time is running out. Let's go inside."

Belladonna sat on the couch while her husband removed her shoes. He touched her soft feet so gently and began to massage her legs. It felt so good the way he touched her. Even though he was a ruthless man in the streets, he always saved his soft side for her, and she loved that she was the only one who saw that side of him. He kissed her thigh and told her how much he loved her. She licked her thick lips as he kissed her.

"Baby, you make me feel so good," she said while moaning.

"You're the reason I do everything I do."

"Really? You would do anything for your lady?"

"You know I would." He grabbed her hand and kissed every finger.

"I want him gone tonight, so stop playing with these fools. He sat on my porch after what he did and had the audacity to offer *our* money back that he stole."

"It'll be done, but you have to stay home."

"No. I want to see this nigga take his last breath. I deserve to see it after what he tried to do to us and your legacy." Belladonna softly pushed Freeway away and stood up.

"I just don't want you to have bad dreams from this shit."

"Freeway, look at me. You don't think I have bad dreams from being snatched up, thrown in a van, and tied up? Allow me a reward from my pain."

He looked at her, walking in a circle, and knew she was in a rage from being taken against her will and used against him as a weakness. Maybe she *did* deserve to see this asshole take his last breath. He just wanted to keep her mental state of mind safe, but he didn't realize that it was already ruined by her being kidnapped.

Freeway got up and wrapped his arms around her. He needed her to know he would protect her no matter what. If he was ruler of New Orleans, she should also feel like a ruler. Belladonna smiled, showing her deep dimples as her husband comforted her with his arms wrapped around her like a security blanket.

"You positive you want to see this, Belladonna?" Freeway had to be sure of her thoughts. He didn't want her to make a decision based on anger.

"I'm positive. I need to know this fool is gone with my own eyes."

"Then I think you need to go prepare yourself and your mind if we're going to do this tonight."

"You can pull the trigger, Freeway. I just want to see him take his last breath."

"I'll handle it, bae."

"I'm going upstairs to take a nap." She kissed him on the forehead and headed for the stairs.

Freeway watched his beautiful wife walk upstairs with her big onion ass and thick thighs moving side to side like the minute hand on an old clock. She had more curves than a country back road. Not realizing it, he was licking his lips. He took a seat on the couch and indulged in his deep thoughts.

He wished he never got her involved in the street life, but he had to admit, he'd rather have her by his side than against him. Belladonna had changed ever since her kidnapping, and he knew that. When something tragic happens to you, you either fold or adapt. He was so proud of how she quickly adapted and didn't let the bad situation collapse her mind-set.

Freeway got off the couch, walked to a nearby closet, and put in a combination that went to a safe behind the closet. The combination was Belladonna's birthdate, of course. Next, he pulled out a 9 mm with a silencer. This was the only weapon he used to eliminate an enemy or an oppressor. He put in a full clip and kissed the handle of the gun. After that, he returned to the couch and sat down, placing the gun on the glass table in front of him.

Freeway dozed off. Four hours had passed. Then his mind woke him up, knowing it was time. He went upstairs and found Belladonna sitting on the edge of the bed dressed in all black. He looked at her with a serious look. She had no smile on her face. She was definitely going through with watching this man die tonight. Freeway stepped inside the walk-in closet and threw on an all-black Polo jogging outfit.

"You serious about this, I see." Freeway broke the silence. "I don't give a fuck what happens. You my husband. If you go down, *I* go down." Belladonna got off the bed and kissed Freeway on the lips with so much passion that to them, it felt like an ocean crashing against the mountains.

Freeway wondered where in hell he would be without this woman. When this was all said and done, he would retire for real just for her, but first, he had to tie up these two dead ends.

They went downstairs and out the front door but not before Freeway grabbed the 9 mm with the silencer, of course. Before getting in the car, Belladonna was curious about one thing and asked,

"Wait a minute. How you suppose to find him?"

"That's easy. I called him earlier and told him I'd spare his life if he brought my money. So, he's going to meet me at my club." Freeway smiled, knowing he had Jackal right where he wanted him . . . like an insect caught in a spider's web.

"Well, let's go." Belladonna jumped into the car with Freeway, and they pulled off.

They rode in silence to the club with their own personal thoughts running through their minds. Belladonna was thinking about the joys of a peaceful mind when all the smoke cleared. Freeway was thinking about him and Belladonna being known as New Orleans rulers. He was going to make sure they would never be tested again. They pulled up to the club and, sure enough, Jackal was already there.

Freeway and Belladonna got out of the car. He unlocked the door and let Jackal walk in first. Jackal was so nervous his palms were sweaty. He set the bags of money down on the bar counter and unzipped one of them, but Freeway stopped him.

"You sure we straight after this?" Jackal stuttered.

"I told you that if you give me money and leave town, you're good." Freeway poured a drink for all three of them.

After having a shot of liquor, Jackal shook Freeway's hand and began to head to the door. He couldn't believe Freeway was going to let him escape and live. Then right when he got to the door, Freeway stopped him.

"Hey, Jackal, aren't you forgetting something?"

"No, what's that?"

"Not once did you apologize to my wife for kidnapping her." Freeway pulled out the 9 mm.

"I humbly apologize, Belladonna. Please, forgive me."

Freeway had no idea that Belladonna had other plans. She looked at Jackal and smiled, then poured another drink for them. They gulped down their drinks. Finished, she unzipped her black hoodie, pulled out a pink Glock, and shot Jackal in the head. His face hit the bar, and he bled out.

"I forgive you, bitch."

"What the fuck?" Freeway was shocked.

"Don't be mad at me, my love, but I had to be the one to take his life."

Chapter 8

Reposition

After Freeway had Jackal's body disposed of, he went back to the house. He badly needed to talk with Belladonna. He felt like he was losing control of her. He never thought in a million years she would pull that trick by killing Jackal her damn self. He understood, but then he didn't understand. He had to get her mind back to the sweet, innocent woman she once was. This was the ignited fire he warned her about.

He ran into the house after parking the car in the garage. Belladonna was sitting in the place watching a movie like nothing ever happened. She was laughing and everything. Freeway walked over, cut off the TV, and slammed the remote on the table. Belladonna was eating popcorn, sitting with her legs crossed and rocking some red panties and a bra. Her chocolate body was glowing. Freeway had to ignore how sexy chocolate she was looking.

"Have you lost your damn mind?" Freeway had never raised his voice at her before.

"What's the problem?"

"That shit you pulled at the club. What was *that* about?"

"I don't see the problem. We agreed on taking him out tonight. The job got done, so what's the big deal?"

"The job got done, Belladonna, but you have to get out of that mind frame. Baby, you not a hired killer."

"I knew if I suggested it, you would say no."

"You disobeyed me."

"Nigga, please." Belladonna got up to go into the kitchen.

Even though Freeway was mad, all he could see was Belladonna's phat, chocolate ass. He stormed into the kitchen, threw her over the table, and pulled her panties to the side. He stuck his dick inside her tight pussy. Then he started slapping her ass. Belladonna knew she was being punished, but this was one punishment she didn't mind at all. She raised her ass in the air as her pussy lips spread open.

Freeway pulled her, demanding she takes all the dick for being a bad girl. Belladonna just kept screaming, "Punish me, daddy." He stuck his thumb in her ass, and she moaned loudly, telling him to stick in more fingers.

"You want to be hardheaded, bitch?"

"Yes, daddy, I been naughty. Fuck me. Come all over my chocolate ass." Belladonna took her hands and spread her butt cheeks.

Freeway was supposed to have been punishing her, but her pussy was so good and wet that he was quickly reaching his climax, so he pulled his dick out and stuck it on her ass. His juices came flushing out of him. Belladonna smiled. His plan of punishing her backfired on him. *She* was the one that punished *him*. She fucked him weak, like the bad bitch he was.

She kissed him and whispered in his ear, "Now, make your lady a drink while I shower." Then she licked his face.

"Fuck, you got it, baby." Freeway knew she would fuck the anger out of him. He knew he had underestimated the power of black pussy.

Freeway had to take multiple drinks for the way Belladonna just put it on him. Good sex or not, he had to get her out of the mind-set that she was in. He knew he had created a monster. The way Belladonna shot Jackal with no hesitation had him wondering.

Freeway ran upstairs and spotted her lying across the bed. He kissed her feet, and she sat up Indian style on the bed.

"You ain't mad at me, right?"

"I'm not mad, but I *am* concerned, bae."

"But why?"

"I don't want blood on your hands or you feeling guilty for killing someone even if they deserve it."

"Have you ever had remorse or guilt, Freeway?"

"To be honest, no. Damn, is that bad?"

"Not really. It's your nature, Freeway. You are a product of your environment. So it's truly under-standable."

"I guess it makes sense, but I don't want that for you. No more killing, Belladonna, I mean it."

"OK, but can you promise me the same thing?"

"Yeah, but after I get rid of Rozay."

"Freeway, I love you and want you out of this life, baby, for me, please."

"I promise you, Belladonna, it will be over soon. I just need you to trust me. When the time comes, you are *not* to pull another trigger."

"OK, I hear you, Freeway."

Belladonna knew Freeway just wanted what was best for her, but she was determined to have his back . . . no matter what.

Freeway kissed her on the cheek and headed to the shower. So many things went through his mind as the hot water hit his body. He thought maybe he should do this alone and not tell her about it, but he knew that would leave her devastated. He knew he had to end this as soon as possible. It was best for their relationship.

If anything was worth him leaving the game for, it was definitely her. He never meant for her to take a life, so what was he thinking? He only wanted her to understand his lifestyle—not live it. What a mess he created, he thought.

He jumped out of the shower, dried off, and put on his Gucci robe. When he stepped back into the bedroom, he noticed that his wife had fallen asleep. As he lay beside her, he kissed her on the lips and held her hand. He had to reposition her mind—and quickly. He didn't want evil thoughts running through her head. He caressed her hair as he pulled her close to him. He would never forgive himself if something happened to his woman. Belladonna was the love of his life, and he did love her more than his money or the streets.

Freeway sat in his car, patiently waiting and watching all the hustlers load into the abandoned building for their daily dice game. He gave off a devilish grin as he loaded up his guns. He warned people repeatedly about stepping on his turf and getting money without his say-so. Since Freeway was known to be a lunatic, everybody tried to tread lightly regarding his turf.

But little did they know, a payoff allowed him to get the information he needed. Grizzly sat in the passenger seat, nervously shaking while watching Freeway's every move. Grizzly was an up-and-coming hustler who dropped out of high school. He'd rather be known as a snitch than go up against the infamous Freeway.

"You not going to tell nobody about our meeting, right, Freeway?"

Freeway looked at Grizzly and slipped out a laugh.

"You little niggas really need to get a backbone, but if I say you good, you good. Now, get the fuck out of my car before somebody sees your scary ass."

Grizzly wasted no time moving. He took the two grand that Freeway gave him and exited the car as quickly as possible. Two grand was a quick come-up to a young buck like him.

When Freeway saw the tall, skinny dice dealer they called Fletcher, he knew that was his cue that the dice game was about to begin. Freeway had warned Fletcher repeatedly not to get money on his turf.

Fletcher thought just because Freeway was dating his sister, Belladonna, that he could constantly get away with the dirt he was doing, but today, Fletcher would learn that he too must follow the rules. As Freeway stepped out of his car, the sun blazed on his mocha skin, reflecting on all his forty-two tattoos. His baby face was the only thing that did not look intimidating on Freeway.

The two young boys guarding the door were so busy talking about the pussy that they would get later that they didn't notice one of the most feared men in New Orleans walking across the street toward them. While Freeway was walking, he screwed on the silencers to his guns. As soon as he hit the sidewalk, he pulled the trigger. The bullet cut straight through the wind making no sounds but a whistle.

Whiff, whiff.

He hit the first young thug in the throat, dropping him to his knees, his hands instantly grabbing his neck. His partner quickly pulled out his gun, not knowing where the bullets came from . . . until he laid his eyes on Freeway.

Freeway didn't even have to tell him to put the gun down because he did so immediately upon seeing him. He tried to take off running, but Freeway's voice stopped him dead in his tracks.

"I wish you *would* and watch me put four shells in your back."

"Come on, Freeway; I'm just a lookout man. I don't get no parts of that money that's getting tossed around in there."

"That's why you going to knock on that door and make them open it. That's the only way I will spare your life."

The boy knew he had no choice, or he would be Freeway's next victim. Freeway stood on the other side of the door while the boy knocked on it. As soon as Freeway heard Fletcher's voice, he pushed the boy out of the way and kicked the door open.

Fletcher fell on the floor as Freeway shut and locked the door behind him. Freeway could not believe the nerve of the five dudes in this room disrespecting his turf like this. Fletcher was too scared to get up, so he just crawled out of Freeway's way.

"That's right, bitch. Don't you move off that floor."

Everybody in the room knew who Freeway was except this one cat who thought he knew it all. He was a high roller from Philly. So everybody just stared at him when he approached Freeway.

"Who the fuck is this dude? How the hell y'all let one nigga come in here and ruin the dice game? Where *I'm* from, we don't let shit fly like this."

"So, where the fuck you from?"

Boom, boom.

Freeway put bullets in the boy's chest before he could even think about saying his name. Then suddenly, Freeway heard somebody coming down the steps, so he quickly ran over and began shooting upstairs.

Fletcher yelled out to Freeway.

"Freeway, stop shooting. That's my sister up there."

"Shut the hell up. You talking about my girl? Why would she be here?"

If there was one person Freeway had a weakness for, it was Belladonna.

She was too nervous about coming downstairs. She didn't want Freeway to know she was there. That's why she got to the dice game early.

"Freeway, please, stop shooting. It's really me up here. Please, stop."

"What the fuck is you doing here, Belladonna?"

"I was counting the money, that's all."

"Have you lost your damn mind? What if a shoot-out had started, and one of these dumb niggas got mad because they lost too much money?"

"My gun is upstairs, Freeway. I'm good because you taught me well. You know that."

When Belladonna reached the last step, Freeway snatched her by her arm and told her to leave and get in his car. Belladonna knew what her man was capable of. She tried to tell her brother to get off the floor, but Freeway advised her to leave.

"I'm not going to tell you but one more time, Belladonna. Get the fuck out of here."

"But—"

"I said go, and I mean *now*."

It was out of her hands. She left her brother in there with the now-raging Freeway.

Pow, pow. Right off the top, Freeway shot two of the dudes in the head and started pacing. Just the thought alone of something happening to Belladonna pissed him off to the third degree. He could not believe Fletcher would be that careless. He turned around and pointed the gun at the last guy's head.

"Who the fuck are you?"

"Listen, man, I just came here to get money. I heard it was a dice game, and I came here to win some money."

"You know, I can't let you leave here. You saw me kill folks . . ."

The guy tried his best to plead his case, but it was too late. Freeway had already pulled the trigger. When Fletcher heard the man's body hit the floor, he began to piss on himself. He knew that he went too far.

Next, Freeway ran over to Fletcher and repeatedly kicked him in the face.

"Have you lost your damn mind, having your sister in this type of bullshit? What the hell is wrong with you?"

"I didn't think it was a big deal. I know these dudes."

"What the fuck is that supposed to mean? Just because you knew these dudes, you think they won't put a bullet in your head?"

The more Freeway talked, the more Fletcher began to see his rage. He could tell Freeway was thinking about killing him. He had to think quickly, but Freeway was already standing over him. The only things that saved Fletcher's life were the gunshots outside the building and the sound of glass shattering.

"Oh shit—Belladonna."

Freeway quickly ran outside, and to his surprise, he saw his car was shot up, and Belladonna was barely crawling in the middle of the street. She was bleeding badly. Freeway dropped down to the ground and scooped her up in his arms.

"Baby, I'm sorry! This is my fault. You're not going to die, not today."

He swiftly put her in the car and drove to Piedmont New Orleans Hospital as fast as he could. Every red light he came to, he shot straight through it. His only concern was getting Belladonna to the hospital in time. After finally reaching the hospital, he carried her into the emergency room. When the hospital staff saw all the blood, they quickly took her out of his arms.

The doctors went to question Freeway, but he had no intention of staying. Instead, he jumped back into his car and returned to the scene of the crime to see if anybody knew anything. His thoughts were clouded as he drove. He could not believe this was happening. It was as if his worst nightmare had become a reality.

When Freeway pulled back up to the abandoned building, he saw Fletcher about to get into a car with somebody. He quickly jumped out and began shooting at the vehicle. The driver immediately jumped out.

"Look, Freeway, I don't know what's going on, but I don't want no problem with you."

Freeway walked over to the passenger side, snatched Fletcher out of the car, and pistol-whipped him repeatedly.

"This is *your* fault. She should never have been here, you careless son of a bitch."

The driver still was standing there watching helplessly, looking scared to death. Finally, Freeway pointed the gun in his direction.

"Why the fuck are you still here? Do you want me to shoot your ass?"

"Hell no, I'm out."

Freeway pulled Fletcher back into the abandoned house, threw him on the cold floor, and forced his gun inside his mouth.

"I should have done this years ago." Freeway pulled the trigger, leaving Fletcher's brains splattered all over the floor.

Then Freeway sat in his car thinking, but he did not know where to start, so he decided to drive to the house of Lazarus, his right-hand man. He always knew the scoop on shit when it went down.

Lazarus was already standing outside when Freeway pulled up. He was from the West Coast but moved to New Orleans when he was young. He and Freeway had been running the streets together ever since. Freeway didn't have to say much because Lazarus had already gotten some info about the news.

"I know what you're feeling right now, Freeway. We have to get to the bottom of this."

"Fuck you mean? I'm ready to murder everything that is moving right now."

"I understand, but we can't make any moves off irrational thinking."

Lazarus's phone began to ring. Two seconds after saying "hello," he handed the phone to Freeway.

"You're not going to believe this, but they asked for you and are using some device to disguise their voice."

"Hello."

"So, how does it feel to be afraid?"

"Who the fuck is this?"

"You been making the streets fear you for a very long time, Freeway. I've noticed that since I've been in your town, but I had to prove people—even you—have a weakness."

"You a fucking coward. Is *that* why you hiding your voice?"

"Shut the fuck up. Your days of running shit are over. I will use your power to get what I want, and if you don't comply, Belladonna will die."

Freeway was not used to being on the receiving end of taking orders. He hated that he was beefing with somebody he could not see, but in this case, he had no choice but to comply.

"What the fuck do you want from me?"

"Word on the streets is that you have a huge empire. I want half of that and half of what you make. So yes, I see the turf you own is a gold mine."

"I don't know how you'll spend it when you're going to be dead."

Lazarus quickly snatched the phone out of Freeway's hand because he could tell the way Freeway was going, he was going to let his ego get the best of him, and that shit was going to get them all killed . . .

Chapter 9

Tasha headed for the break room. She was tired from working her other job and knew if she did not get some coffee in her, she would not make it through the day. What she really needed was a shot of Hennessy. She couldn't believe that she had left the street life alone to work *two* jobs, staying tired with low pay, but she promised her little sister she would change her lifestyle.

While making a cup of coffee, her coworker came rushing into the break room.

"Damn, Tasha, are you OK? How are you feeling?"

"Girl, what the hell are you talking about now? Can't you see I'm trying to make some coffee?"

"Oh shit, you don't know, do you?"

"Know what? I just got here."

"Tasha, how the hell you the head nurse and don't know that your baby sister has been shot?"

The cup of coffee fell out of Tasha's hand, hitting the floor. The news she had just heard felt like a ton of bricks had landed on her shoulders. The

first thing she tried to do was call Freeway, but he
didn't answer. Now, she really was panicking.

Her coworker grabbed her by the hand and
led her to her sister's room. In the middle of the
hospital, Tasha stopped and jerked away from her
coworker.

"Just tell me right now. Is my sister dead or
alive?"

"Honestly, I don't know, Tasha. You're the head
nurse, and they would tell you before they'd tell
me. Now, let's go."

Going down the hallway, all she could think
about was how the hell could Freeway allow this to
happen. He always kept a good eye on Belladonna.
But she knew one thing for sure . . . If her sister
died, she would jump back into the street and get
answers and kill Freeway in the process for letting
this happen.

"Tasha, that's the doctor right there who was
working on your sister."

Tasha headed over to him and asked about her
sister.

"Well, as of right now, she has slipped into a
coma. So all we can do is hope for the best."

The news made Tasha light-headed. She almost
hit the floor before her coworker caught her. The
doctor told her to get some ice. When she returned
with the ice pack, she held it on Tasha's head. After

twenty minutes, Tasha began to take off all her nursing gear and tossed it on the floor.

"Tasha, what are you doing? Are you okay?"

"I hope your ass is not pregnant," barked Tasha.

Brenda laughed at her, thinking she was going crazy because of the news she just heard. But when she looked at Tasha's face, she could see that she was *very* serious.

"What a minute. You are serious. Please tell me you are not serious."

"I'm afraid so. I only gave it up for my little sister, but I need to get to the bottom of this."

"But your job—"

"Fuck this job, Brenda."

Brenda no longer recognized this Tasha. She slightly dropped her head. Tasha only felt bad because she knew Brenda was a square and knew nothing about street life, so she explained it the best way she could but did not tell her too much.

"I used to kill people for money and had no problem doing it. But ironically, my biggest nemesis was my sister's fiancé."

"Freeway? But he seems so nice."

Tasha gave a little laugh because she knew Brenda was naïve to the behaviors of a silent killer.

"Trust and believe, Freeway is a snake in the grass and a stone-cold killer. Both he and his sneaky friend Lazarus."

At one point in life, Tasha and Freeway were the best friends, but when her best friend got murdered, she knew Lazarus was behind it, and she got pissed at Freeway for sticking up for him. So that put the two of them at odds.

"Well, listen, I got to go, but keep me updated on my sister, will you?"

"Tasha, I know we don't know each other well, but be safe."

Tasha was the type of person who did not know how to show love, so she just smiled and walked off. But knowing what she had to do to get the news and information she wanted, she knew she could not be weak. Her priority was to find that damn Freeway and question him.

Freeway and Lazarus

Lazarus took over the conversation. He felt he could get things done a lot better than how Freeway was doing. Freeway stood by and waited, but he did not like how Lazarus conducted business over the phone. To him, it just sounded like he agreed to everything. Finally, Lazarus got off the phone and explained to Freeway what would take place.

"We have to rob the Gambino brothers by tomorrow—or else."

"What the fuck do me robbing them Italian motherfuckers got to do with my wife?"

"He knows the power you have, Freeway. So he's going to use your power and muscle to get some bread out of this."

"Why the fuck does it sound like you're a spokesman for this fool? Whose side are you on?"

Lazarus had to be careful with the words he chose because he knew Freeway was a trigger-happy, murdering fool, and with the rage he was feeling at that moment, he, himself, could even get murdered.

"I'm just saying, Freeway, we need to handle this as soon as possible if we want to get a step closer to handling this fool."

"I'm going to tell you right now—whoever this dude is, when this is all over with, I'm going to kill him regardless of whether you're down."

Freeway kept feeling his phone vibrating in his pocket. He pulled it out with anger and anticipation. When he saw who had been calling him, he knew there were about to be some serious problems. He decided to call her back to get the conversation over with. Tasha picked up the phone on the first ring.

"It's about damn time. I know you see me calling you."

"Tasha, I don't have time for your drama. I have bigger problems right now."

"You damn right you have big problems, *especially* if my sister dies. Then your *real* problems have just begun," she warned.

Freeway hung up the phone. He did not have time to argue with Tasha over some old beef. The only thing that mattered to him was getting the job done of robbing the Gambino brothers. This would not be an easy task, not even for him. Those brothers did not play when it came to their money, and they damn sure did not trust Blacks.

Freeway instructed Lazarus to get in the car. Lazarus popped his trunk and pulled out his double-barreled shotgun. It seemed funny to Freeway how Lazarus looked like he was already prepared for this situation. Lazarus threw his gun in the backseat. When he jumped in the passenger side, he could feel the intensity and frustration of Freeway's eyes staring at him.

"What's the problem? Why are you looking at me like *I'm* the bad guy?"

"I can't help but notice that you are so prepared for this situation. You wanted to try to rob and take over the Gambino organization two years ago, but I told you it would be too much of a hassle."

"Now you see? We should have robbed them ourselves, but now, we have to give the money to this jerk."

As they pulled up to the Gambino restaurant, Freeway gave Lazarus simple instructions because he knew how flashy his partner could be. He needed Lazarus to be on point and not play around because the Gambino brothers would shoot to kill first and ask questions later.

"This is not a joke, Lazarus. You know how these motherfuckers are. A lot of niggas died trying to run up in this spot, so we need to be on point."

"Trust and believe. I got you."

"Because your shotgun is so obvious, wait a few minutes, then come inside blasting. By that time, I'll have already set it off. I need you to have my back on this."

"Handle your business, Freeway. You know you can trust me."

Nervous, Freeway walked in. He knew the Gambino brothers were ruthless. You don't just walk in and rob these types of dudes. You have to prepare for it, but Freeway had few options and no time to prepare. He had no choice but to handle the situation or die trying.

When he walked into the building, low, soft jazz music was playing in the background. The brothers were already sitting at a table meeting with three other guys.

The bodyguard went to frisk Freeway to see if he had any guns on him, but the older brother, Carlo, waved him off. The two brothers, Carlo and Lucky, looked alike, except Carlo was fat, and Lucky was skinny. Everybody at the table knew exactly who Freeway was. Freeway's presence made a couple of guys at the table nervous. They knew he was a killer, for sure. Lucky took it upon himself to offer Freeway a plate and seat.

"My good friend, Freeway, we will be with you in a minute," smiled Lucky.

Freeway was one of the few Black people that the Gambino brothers liked, but all that was about to change—and far worse than that because Freeway knew he would have to kill the two brothers or else he would always be looking over his shoulder. Freeway pulled out his gun. Carlo took notice and stood up.

"Freeway, my friend, this had better be a joke."

"I wish this were, but I have no choice, Carlo," Freeway said with an uncomfortable look on his face. Lucky could tell whatever it was, Freeway really did not want to do it and felt he had no choice. Lucky tried his best to reason with him.

"This is not like you, Freeway. We have a great business relationship. Whatever it is, we can handle this and find a solution."

"I need everything you got in the safe, Lucky. Please don't make me ask you twice."

Just to let Carlo and Lucky know he was not playing, he shot one of the men at the table in the back of the head.

Pow, pow.

"That's it, Freeway! You have one more chance to put down your gun," Carlo said angrily, standing up.

"Sit the fuck down, Carlo. Don't make me shoot you," Freeway ordered.

"Whatever this is, we can work it out."

Freeway did not think they were getting the message, so he shot the other two guys at the table. Finally, the bodyguard had seen enough and pulled out his gun and pointed it at Freeway. Freeway laughed at him because he saw the fear in his eyes. The bodyguard's hand was shaking. He never thought in a million years that somebody would really try to kill Carlo or Lucky. That's the only reason he took the job.

"Listen, young buck, put down your gun. This has nothing to do with you."

"Can't do that. I have to protect my bosses."

"Fine then. You can share a coffin with them too."

Freeway shot the boy in the head twice; he never saw it coming. Then Lucky saw that there were no more bodies alive to protect them. With no other option, he quickly picked up his phone to call for his assault team, but it was too late. Freeway had already made it to him and pressed the tip of his shotgun under Lucky's chin.

"I told you we could have just done this the easy way," Freeway said with a sadistic grin.

Chapter 10

Carlo had his hands up in the air, looking at Freeway press his gun as hard as he could under Lucky's chin. Carlo threatened Freeway one more time, hoping he would change his mind about the situation.

"Freeway, you still have a chance, but if you rob us, you know we have no choice but to kill you. We gave you and Brasco a pass on the Alfredo hit."

"I know, Carlo. That's why I will not leave here until you two are dead."

Freeway could not help but mutter to himself, "Where the fuck is Lazarus?"

He could have died if he wasn't quick on his feet, but little did Freeway know . . . it was about to get worse.

Suddenly, a rain of bullets ripped through the kitchen door, forcing Freeway to run and jump behind the bar. The bullets came too fast, and by how they hit the bar's back wall, he could tell the guy was shooting an M16.

All Freeway could think about was . . . What the hell had he gotten into, and where the hell was Lazarus? Lucky and Carlo grabbed their guns. They were not going to take any more chances with Freeway.

"You have nowhere to run, so you might as well come out, Freeway," Lucky said with a vengeful tone.

"I'm not going to die here, Lucky. You and Carlo are."

Lucky could not believe Freeway still had the balls to say something like that, even though they had him cornered.

He gave the signal to his hit man, who was holding the assault rifle, to continue shooting. While the hit man went to reload his clip, Lazarus finally kicked in the door and shot the guy twice in his chest with his pump shotgun. When Freeway heard the pump, that was all the leverage he needed. He jumped over the bar countertop and shot Carlo in the face.

"Put down your fucking gun, Lucky, right now," Freeway said in a victorious voice. Lucky immediately dropped his gun as he saw the odds were against him, and he had no chance of defeating Freeway and Lazarus. He began to talk in a low, weak voice.

"Why are you doing this, Freeway? I have been nothing but loyal to you on the business end."

"I told you this was not personal. It's business, so please don't take it personally when I kill you."

"Whatever this is about, I'm sure I can fix this or whoever has hired you. So let me double it."

Lazarus took it upon himself to hit Lucky in the stomach with his gun and force him down on his knees. As soon as Freeway was about to ask Lucky where the money was, he heard a voice that pissed him off even more.

"Well, look what we have here. Why didn't you invite me to the party, Freeway? And I should have known that you would be here, Lazarus," Tasha said as she walked in with her gun.

Freeway did not need to turn around to know who it was. It was the one person he did not feel like dealing with at that moment. Lazarus gave Freeway a look as if to ask, "What is she doing here?""Don't give him that look, Lazarus, because I still owe your ass a bullet. As soon as I prove you killed my homegirl, your ass is mine, and Freeway won't be able to save you."

"Do you think that I fear you, Tasha? Honestly, you don't faze me," Lazarus said while pointing his shotgun at her.

"Both of y'all shut the fuck up. I don't have time to deal with this right now," Freeway said while waving his gun in the air and putting his attention back on Lucky.

Freeway was tired of playing games with Lucky, so he kicked him dead in the face, sending his limp body crashing to the floor. Lazarus put the shotgun to the back of Lucky's head, but Freeway got tired of Lazarus thinking he was running things, so he pushed Lazarus back.

"Did you forget who the fuck is running shit around here? You better wake up and stop playing yourself, Lazarus. You hear me? Do you fucking *hear* me?"

"I hear you. Damn." No matter how much Lazarus hated being embarrassed in front of Tasha, he was no fool. He was not going to challenge a raging Freeway. Freeway picked up Lucky and repeatedly slammed his head to the floor.

"I am going to ask you one more time—where fuck is the money?" Lucky was so weak from the loss of blood he couldn't speak. So he just pointed to the back toward the kitchen. Tasha went to check, but Freeway stopped her in her tracks.

"Where the fuck do you think you're going?"

"I'm going to search for the money."

"Says who? I don't trust you, Tasha. You stand right there where I can see you. Lazarus, go search for the money."

"Oh, that's right. It would be better if you send your personal bitch," Tasha said with a big smile, looking in Lazarus's direction.

"Nigga, what the fuck is you waiting for? Don't listen to her. Go look for the money," Freeway said in a very agitated voice.

He was tired of playing around. He needed to hurry up and check on his wife. He realized that he had wasted way too much time in the restaurant.

"Freeway, you're going pay for this with your life," Lucky said in a weak voice.

Freeway smashed his face to the floor again for the threat he had just mumbled. Lazarus returned with four big bags of money and a smile to match.

When Freeway saw that, he stood up and cocked his gun while flipping Lucky's body over so Lucky could look at his face.

"I don't want you to think that I'm a coward, Lucky, so I want you to look at me while I shoot you."

Lucky had no more words left. He knew Freeway was not backing off. He slowly closed his eyes.

*Pow, pow.*After shooting Lucky twice in the head, Freeway stared at him for a moment, wishing that it had not come down to him dying, But God knew that he had no choice. Lazarus was about to dump all the money on the table until Freeway pulled out his gun.

"What the fuck are you doing with that money? It's not for us to keep. Matter of fact, get that bastard on the phone and tell him that the job's done."

Lazarus zipped up the duffle bag again and called the unknown caller. After answering the phone, he told Lazarus to pass the phone to Freeway.

"Job well done, Freeway. Not just any person could have walked into the Gambino brothers' place and pulled off what you just did. Give the phone back to your partner, so I can tell him where to drop off the money, but in the meantime, stay close to that phone because I got two more jobs for you."

"No—fuck that! I'm not going to keep doing this job. Show me your face, you fucking coward," Freeway said while looking at the phone as he held it as if the guy could see him.

Tasha ran over and jerked the phone out of his hand.

"Nigga, is you crazy? You're going to get my little sister killed. We don't even know who this guy is, so he can have anybody walk into that hospital and kill Belladonna. Think, Freeway—think."

As much as Freeway hated to admit it, Tasha was right. He was not used to taking orders from anybody. He was always the big fish and called the shots. He gave Tasha a hand gesture for her to take over the call, and that's precisely what she did. She could tell by the look on Lazarus's face that he did not like that one bit, but this was about *her* sister, so she could care less.

"Listen, we got your money. Where do you want us to drop it off at?" Tasha said in a calm but stern voice.

"How ironic. A bitch that wants to take charge. How far are you from the post office?"

"Not that far. Maybe like fifteen minutes tops."

"Good. Go there now, and I'll have somebody meet you there, but Freeway must stay in the car. I don't trust him."

Tasha hung up the phone. She could tell whoever the guy was, he feared Freeway and knew how dangerous he could be. She told them the plan as they exited the building with the money. Tasha went to get in Freeway's car, but he shut her door as she opened it.

"Where the hell do you think you're going?"

"Freeway, Belladonna may be your woman, but that is *my* sister, so you can kill that noise you talking. Besides, you need me."

"Need you? Please, don't make me laugh. Why would I need you? Have you forgotten who I am?"

"No, I have not forgotten who you are, and neither has that person on the phone," Tasha said as she pushed his hand away to open the door.

"What the hell is that supposed to mean?" Freeway said as he closed the door again and stood in front of it this time. Lazarus sat back and laughed at them. He could not believe the rivalry the two had going on. Actually, Lazarus was jealous of their relationship. He knew deep inside that Tasha and Freeway were not close anymore because of him.

No matter how much Tasha said she would kill Freeway, he knew that would never happen because of the closeness the two once shared, but Freeway, on the other hand . . . he really didn't know about. Freeway was always unpredictable.

"I tell you what. You two handle this, and I'll be in the car," Lazarus said while getting in the backseat with the money.

"I'm telling you right now, Freeway, whoever this guy is on the phone, he fears you. So, when we get to the post office, you cannot get out of this car. Is that understood?" Tasha said while crossing her arms and waiting for Freeway's unpredictable response.

"You know what? Fuck it. Let's go so we can get this over with," he said while snatching the driver's door open. He was tired of bickering with Tasha. At that moment, his only concern was Belladonna.

While driving down the road, Freeway wanted to get something off his chest. He had to let Tasha know that she was not running a damn thing but her mouth. He glanced over at her and thought, *Look at her thinking she's a boss.* Finally, he could not take it anymore. He had to bust her bubble. But little did he know, Tasha could already feel his ego getting the best of him, so she beat him to the punch.

"Freeway, why the fuck do you think somebody is always trying to run over the top of you?"

"Because you are, Tasha. I understand Belladonna is your baby sister. But you just came in the mix and have been trying to take over ever since."

"You are so wrong, Freeway. I *had* to step in. Your ego is going to get us all killed," she said while shifting her mind to the transaction they were about to make.

She knew she had to focus on observing everything they were about to do regarding this drop-off.

They all unbuckled their seat belts and prepared themselves as they pulled into the post office parking lot.

Chapter 11

At the post office, Freeway was looking around for anything suspicious. But to his surprise, everything looked like a regular mail-moving day. So he parked right in front of the post office to see all the movement and activity going on inside. He did not want to get caught off guard.

Lazarus rolled down his window and enjoyed the cool breeze coming through it. Tasha glanced in the mirror and saw how calm he was, and she did not like it one bit, and she damn sure was about to turn around and let him know about it.

"Lazarus, why the fuck are you so damn calm?"

"Tasha, don't start with me. Just turn around."

"Fuck that. Why are you so calm?"

"You must want me, don't you, Tasha?" Lazarus said while licking his lips, looking at her, which insulted her. She reached between her legs, grabbed her gun, and reached into the backseat, pointing it at his head. She began to lick her lips as well. While she pressed the tip of her gun against Lazarus's head, she dared him to smile or even speak.

"Look at you. I can see the bitch coming out of you now," she said with a devious grin, making her appear like the female Grinch. But her fun ended when the phone in the middle console started ringing. Tasha went to pick it up, but Freeway snatched it out of her hand with an uncertain look on his face. She raised her hands in the air as if to say, "You got it."

"We got your money. Now show yourself," Freeway growled.

"See, this is the problem, Freeway. You think you run the show, but you don't run nothing. I got people in the hospital watching your precious Belladonna, so don't play with me. Give the phone to the bitch, or the deal is off."

Freeway threw the phone in Tasha's lap while punching the steering wheel. He was sick of these reindeer games. Tasha looked at the phone, then looked at Freeway. She was confused. Freeway snapped at her for acting like she didn't know what was happening.

"Bitch, pick up the phone. You acted like you were running shit earlier, so handle this shit before I start shooting motherfuckers."

Tasha quickly picked up the phone as she saw the rage in Freeway's eyes build. Not even she would test him at this point. She calmly answered.

The unknown caller said while inserting laughter behind his statement, "Tasha, I'm warning you right now, if the person picking up the money is harmed in any way, your sister dies."

"How the hell do you know my name?"

Knock, knock.

Tasha's attention was drawn to the tapping on her window. Immediately, the phone slipped out of her hand when she realized who was standing on the other side of the window. She immediately swung open the door with her gun in her hand. She threw the girl tapping on her window onto the hood of the car face-first and pressed her pistol against the back of her head.

"Brenda, what the hell are you doing here? What is this about?" Tasha gritted through her teeth.

"You know what this is about, Tasha. It's about you and Freeway. How y'all both been getting away with a lot of shit. Now, it's time for you to run us our money, or Belladonna will pay with her life."

"Bitch, I should blow your brains out right now."

"Do it—and Belladonna dies," she reminded her.

Freeway knew he was ordered to stay in the car, but he wanted to jump out so badly to see what was happening. He could see the issue but not quite hear it. Tasha, realizing she had no choice, released Brenda, who got off the hood of the car with a smirk on her face.

"As I said, you and Freeway have gotten away with a lot of dirt in the streets. But do you *really* think that all is forgiven just because you became

a nurse, Tasha? So, today, you two will pay up—or
else . . . Now, if you don't mind, I'll take the money."

Tasha knocked on Lazarus's side of the window
so he could get out and make the transaction.
While he took the money to Brenda's car, she
broke down the rules for their next job. Now,
Brenda signaled for Freeway to get out of the car,
and he wasted no time doing so.

"First of all, this has nothing to do with Lazarus.
This is all about you and Tasha, Freeway. This is
your judgment day, *not* his. So, for the next two
jobs, you and Tasha will work alone, or Belladonna
will die, understood?"

"Why the fuck are you running the show? You're
no boss," Tasha said, still holding her gun tightly.

"Tasha, you aren't running things. *I* am, and if
you don't comply, Belladonna is dead. If you touch
me, Belladonna is dead. Now, down to business.
Your next job is to shut down Kurupt, take everything he has, and bring it to me. But we'll be fair.
We know this is a tough job, so we'll give you 10
percent, but we need proof that he is dead."

Tasha looked at Freeway, and they both knew
they were being set up. Going after Kurupt was
suicidal. Whoever was planning all of this knew
Kurupt was the only man in New Orleans who
did not fear Freeway. He and Freeway were first
cousins, and their moms were sisters. They agreed
not to beef with or step on each other's toes or

territory. Tasha realized that this would be a hard pill for Freeway to swallow.

"When this is over, you *know* we're going to kill you, right?" Tasha said with a vengeful look in her eyes.

"Trust and believe, Tasha, when this is all over, I will be long gone, and my partners and I will be rich. So will you if you play the game."

The phone Freeway was holding began vibrating. He immediately answered it because he already knew who it was. He spoke through the phone with hatred and anger and was ready to kill whoever was on the other end of the line.

"You a fucking coward to send a bitch to do your job. As soon as you show your face, I will personally put a bullet in your forehead."

"Now, Freeway, is that any way to talk to the person who has power over your woman? If I were you, I would calm down—and I mean *now.*"

Freeway hung up the phone and told Tasha to get into the car. He did not want to waste any more time. He figured that he might as well get it over with. Lazarus started running to the car, but Freeway stopped him.

"You can't come with us. It's forbidden," Freeway said as he climbed in and quickly hit reverse, speeding out of the parking lot. As he headed to one of his secret spots, Tasha wondered if Freeway noticed how strange Lazarus was acting.

"You know I don't like Lazarus, but, Freeway, you have to admit he was acting really strange about this whole situation," she said. But as usual, Freeway brushed her off.

"You just tripping because you don't like him. You notice every little fault about him."

"I'm telling you, Freeway, shit just ain't right with that nigga."

Freeway ignored her as he pulled into one of the grimiest projects in New Orleans. This made Tasha mad, not because she was afraid of the projects but because she had so many enemies, and being there wouldn't work out in her favor if something went south. So she started to tell Freeway about it, but he cut her off.

"Listen, Freeway, I don't think—"

"Don't worry about it. You with me, so you know that nobody will try you out here as long as we're together."

The whole apartment complex was shaped in one big square . . . one way in, and one way out. They got out of the car and walked down the sidewalk. Tasha could feel people looking in her direction. She pulled out her gun, but Freeway quickly took it out of her hand.

"You don't need this. I got you," he said as he tucked her gun underneath his shirt. Tasha was amazed at how everybody moved out of his way.

Freeway had made a name for himself, and you could tell that as he walked through the crowd. It did not dawn on Tasha who she had been beefing with for the last couple of years. Freeway was a kingpin.

Freeway reached his building, and the boys there who were rolling dice quickly picked up the money and moved, but Freeway did not. The young boys were nervous. They knew Freeway had warned them about shooting dice there. It drew too much attention to his building. The reason Freeway lasted so long in the game was that he never brought attention to himself or the people around him.

Before one of the young boys could explain himself, Freeway grabbed him by his throat.

"What the fuck did I tell you about shooting dice in front of my spot? What the fuck did I tell you?"

"You said not to shoot dice where your money rests at," the young boy said with tears rolling down his face.

The other little hustlers were about to run when he pulled out his gun. Freeway told them they better not take a step, or they would all be shot in the back. Tasha knew Freeway was a live wire, but she did not think he could be this devious.

"I want you to get on your knees and place your right hand flat on the pavement, and I want your friends to watch," Freeway said while putting a brand-new clip in his gun.

"Please, Freeway, please, don't." The young boy cried out for mercy.

"Shut the fuck up and be a man."

Pow, pow, pow.

Freeway shot the boy in his hand three times. Then he stepped on the injured hand while the boy cried in agony. Finished, Freeway bent over and put the gun to the boy's head while gripping the back of his neck.

"Take a really good look around. Nobody is going to help you. *I* run all of this, and the next time I tell you to do something, you better fucking do it. Do I make myself clear?"

The young boy nodded as Freeway let him go. Then as they were walking into the building, a little girl ran up to the boy, hugged him, asked if he was OK, and said she was sorry for saying she was hungry. At that moment, Freeway understood why the boy was defiant and rolled the dice anyway. He was only trying to feed his little sister.

When Freeway pulled out his gun, the first thing Tasha thought was that he would shoot the boy. Then the little girl saw Freeway walking in their direction and became frightened because she knew of Freeway and what he might do.

Freeway reached down and pulled the boy up by his collar, gave him the same gun he used to shoot him in the hand, reached into his pocket, and gave him five grand.

"Now, get a doctor to fix you up and feed your sister. I better not ever see you out here struggling again," Freeway said as he walked away and signaled for Tasha to follow him inside the building.

Chapter 12

As they walked through the apartment building hallway, Tasha could not help but see all the lost souls. So many people were strung out on drugs, and many kids played in the hallway with no parents around. Likely, their parents were somewhere getting high. Tasha couldn't believe the kingpin—the almighty Freeway—lived there.

They finally reached Freeway's door. He unlocked it and walked inside. Tasha could not believe how his apartment looked. The outside of it was a low-budget, drug-infested building. However, inside was a pricy spotless Russian white carpet, expensive wallpaper, mirrors plastered around the whole living room, and a seventy-inch TV.

Tasha wondered why Freeway would have all this in such a run-down, crime-ridden building . . . and then she remembered the type of guy he was. She quickly rid her mind of such thoughts. She didn't have the nerve to ask him, but Freeway could read the expression on her face.

"I know what you're thinking . . . Why would I pick a place like this to lay my head? Truth be told, I don't stay here, but I have some important things that do."

"Let me guess . . . Your drugs and guns are here," Tasha said with a sarcastic look like she knew the answer.

"Something like that. You know, Tasha, we've been beefing for a while. You repeatedly told me how you would kill me and even shot up my car."

"Well, you know how it is when your emotions are high," she said, looking a little nervous.

"But here we are, about to do a job together."

Tasha sat down on the couch, feeling a little better now that she had heard how calm Freeway sounded. He turned on the TV, then went to his closet to get his guns. He pulled out a duffle bag and placed it on the couch beside her. Tasha wasted no time digging through the bag. While she was admiring all the nice guns he had, she noticed something about them. None of them had bullets or clips in them.

Tasha turned around to ask Freeway where the bullets were, but her words died in her throat when she saw that Freeway had a gun pointed at her. Now, she realized why he had taken her weapon. The same gun he took from her was now pointed at her head. Freeway shook his head.

"Come on, Tasha, did you *really* think you were going to get away with shooting me?" he asked as he walked closer to the couch.

"Come on, Freeway. I thought we had just resolved this."

"No, *you* resolved this."

"But—"

"Shut the fuck up. Your time is up. I just didn't want Belladonna to know how badly I wanted to kill you."

"You *need* me, Freeway. You need me to help you with these jobs to save my sister's life," she said as she stood but kept her hands in the air.

"I *don't* need you. People fear me, so I already have the upper hand when I walk into a room."

"Freeway—"

*Pow, pow, pow.*Freeway emptied his clip into Tasha's chest. He was tired of delaying a murder he should have taken care of long ago. After that, he grabbed the duffle bag, put two assault rifles in it, pulled out his phone, and called his cleanup man to come and remove the body from his apartment.

Freeway then called Kurupt to set up a mock meeting about partnering up. Of course, this was music to Kurupt's ears. He had always wanted to partner with his cousin, but Freeway always wanted to be his own boss and answer only to himself.

As Freeway was walking out of the apartment, he remembered the last encounter he had with his cousin and how he tried so hard to get him to join his team, but they fell out on bad terms when Freeway had to show one of Kurupt's favorite hittas why he was his own boss.

"It's about time we all pulled together and became one happy team. We can all get the money, so I'm glad all the bosses could come out and support," Kurupt said, pouring a glass of Grey Goose.

"Well, it seems to me that not all of us are bosses," Freeway said as he took off his shades and looked dead at Kurupt's right-hand man, Blaze.

"Why the fuck are you looking at me, Freeway?" Blaze said as he stood up, but Kurupt quickly made him sit down because he knew his man didn't stand a chance going against his cousin, Freeway.

"Because I can. Pussy, you know better than to ever step on my territory. That goes for everybody at this table. You all know better than to step on my turf."

The seven other members knew not to say anything to Freeway because they feared him and knew he was a killer. But Kurupt did not like how his cousin was striking so much fear in everybody for the simple reason this made people do business with Freeway.

"Calm down. We are all family here, Freeway."

"No-no. Correction, you and I are family here, but everybody else is just here, Kurupt. So why in the hell did I even come here? I have shit to do."

Kurupt could see there was no chill button on his cousin's drama, so he said, "Freeway, you leave me with no choice. Either tone yourself down, or you cannot be part of my organization. Now, I hate to have to say that because we're blood, but business is business."

"Fuck your organization."

"Freeway, it does not have to be like this."

"You just made it like this. I grind hard and made these millions on my own. None of these fake-ass niggas were there."

"Freeway, you know if you are not part of my organization, then you are part of the problem."

"Tell you what, Kurupt. You don't want this problem with me, and since you're family, how about I don't step on your turf, and you don't step on mine?" As he spoke, Freeway looked at all the scared faces around the table.

"Fine, Freeway, but I hope we don't have an issue."

"*For your sake, I hope not,*" Freeway said as he got out of his chair and proceeded to leave the meeting.

"*Where the fuck do you think you're going, Freeway?*" Blaze questioned angrily.

Then Kurupt said calmly but firmly, "*Sit down, Blaze.*"

"*That's right. Be a good little bitch and sit down like your boss told you to,*" Freeway said with a mocking smile.

As Freeway walked by Blaze, Blaze picked up Kurupt's glass of liquor and threw it in Freeway's face. Everybody at the table knew that Blaze had just made the biggest mistake of his life. Kurupt sat down. He knew he would not be able to interfere in what was to follow. It's one thing family never did. They never picked sides and went against each other.

Freeway wiped the liquor out of his eyes, and before Blaze could blink his eyes, Freeway had already pulled out his pistol and smacked him upside his head. He then slammed him face-first on the table. Now his gun was pressed to the back of Blaze's head so hard that he begged for mercy. The other members knew what would go down, so they all quickly got up and left.

"*You guys sure you don't want to say your last goodbyes to this bitch?*" Freeway said while repeatedly smacking Blaze in the back of his head.

"*Freeway, that's enough,*" *Kurupt said, standing up and pushing his cousin away.*

"*So, you pick this nigga over me? After you just saw him disrespect me? This is how we doing each other now?*" *Freeway said while tucking away his gun.*

"*You are doing too much. I'm trying my best not to beef with you.*"

"*Beef with me? I don't think you want to do that.*"

"*You can't come in here and disrespect my organization and my right-hand man.*"

"*Fuck this nigga right here. For all you know, he could be plotting to take over your little organization.*"

"*What you need to be worried about, Freeway, is how to keep Tasha from shooting up your whips. Oh yeah, I heard about that.*"

"*So, you think that's funny, huh, Kurupt?*" *Freeway said as he pulled out his gun again. Kurupt saw the look in Freeway's eyes, so he pulled out his steel.*

Pow, pow.

Kurupt turned around and shot Blaze in the head. He didn't want Freeway to have any leverage over him. "*What now, Freeway?*"

"*I'm just glad you got your balls back. Keep your niggas off my turf . . . or else,*" *Freeway said as he once again tucked his gun away and walked from Kurupt, heading for the door.*

Then Kurupt called out to Freeway, "Or else what?"

"Or else we will have this meeting again, but next time, it won't be you doing the shooting."

Freeway snapped out of his daydream as he reached his car. He did not think that the last words he would say to his cousin would come true now that he really had to kill his own flesh and blood. But before driving to Kurupt's house, Freeway decided to stop by the hospital to check on Belladonna. After asking the receptionist about her room number, he headed that way.

When he reached her room, he closed the door behind him, hoping she was still alive. In his opinion, the fact that she still had a room in the hospital was a good thing. It meant that she was still breathing.

However, when Freeway stepped into the room and looked at the bed, he was shocked to see that Belladonna was not there. When he went to find out what was happening, the door opened, and Brenda walked in.

"Now, how did I know I was going to find *you* here, Freeway?" she said while closing the door behind her. "You never said I could not come to see her," he replied.

"You're right, but you did not ask either."

Freeway was sick of this woman thinking she was a boss and running things. He quickly pulled out his gun. "Where is she?"

"Now, Freeway, you know you cannot put your hands on me."

"*Where* is she?" he repeated.

"Don't worry, Freeway. She's safe."

Freeway grabbed Brenda by her hair and stuck his gun beneath her chin. Brenda was terrified because she knew how dangerous he was. She tried to jerk away, but his grip was far too tight.

"You kill me, Freeway, and you will *never* see Belladonna again."

Freeway whispered in her ear, "I don't know what you heard about me, but I will body your ass right here. I need to know if she's okay."

"Let me get into my pocket to make a phone call." She slowly pulled out her phone and made a call. Freeway heard her tell the person to send her the pictures, so he loosened his grip on her. She showed Freeway the photos of his wife being well taken care of.

Finally, he let Brenda go and went to handle his business with Kurupt.

Chapter 13

Freeway sat across the street from his cousin's mini-mansion. He was so pissed off that he allowed himself to be put in a position where somebody had power over him. He watched all the guards who were protecting his cousin's property. Freeway felt Kurupt was a fool for being so sloppy and flashy. Not in a million years would Freeway be caught dead spending money on a mansion. In his eyes, that was a bad investment.

He took another sip of Grey Goose. He could not believe the day had come when he would bring down his cousin's whole compound. He knew he had to do this right—cousin or no cousin. He knew Kurupt would clap back if his back were against the wall.

Freeway picked up his gun from the passenger seat and inserted a full clip. Before getting out of the car, he took another sip of his liquid courage. On purpose, he left the duffle bag in his car so he would have a reason to return to the vehicle. He walked up the sidewalk leading to Kurupt's house.

On either side of the walkway was a small garden with strawberry bushes.

"Stop right there! Turn around, nice and slow."

"Do you know who I am?"

"Shut up. I know who you are."

"I think it would be in *your* best interest to put down the gun."

"I said, shut up."

"You *do* know you just committed suicide, right?" Freeway said as he turned around in a full circle so he could see the gunman's eyes. When the other guard standing by the door saw who his partner had his gun pointed at, he rushed over to his side and resolved the issue before it got worse.

"What are you doing? Do you know who this is?"

"I don't give a fuck who it is. I know his face, and he's nothing but trouble."While the two argued about the situation, Freeway swiftly removed the knife he held in his back pocket and stabbed the gunman in the throat, and in a quick motion, caught his gun before his body even hit the ground.

"I have nothing but respect for you, Freeway," the remaining guard said while throwing his hands in the air.

"How long have you been working for my cousin?"

"Not long; maybe a year."

"Do you like it here?"

"Yes, it's OK," the guard replied, his voice cracking from nervousness as he answered the question.

"Be a man; be honest."

"I think Kurupt pays too much favoritism, but he's a powerful man, so I play my part."

"I'm going to give you one chance—and only one chance—to walk off this compound because I'm about to go to war with my cousin."

The guy looked at Freeway as if he were joking. He started laughing because, in his mind, he felt like he was being set up, and maybe his loyalty was being tested, so he did not move. Freeway started counting backward from five: "Five, four, three—"

The guard's smile instantly disappeared—and so did he. He took off running in a zigzag motion just in case Freeway changed his mind and started shooting. Freeway laughed at how he was running. Then he turned around and focused on the task looming before him. Truth be told, what was about to go down between Kurupt and him would *not* be a laughing matter.

Freeway walked into Kurupt's mansion, and as he stepped onto the impressive all-red marble floor, the first thing he thought was that it was too bad his cousin's blood would soon be spilled, desecrating the luxurious Calacatta marble floor.

"Cousin, Cousin, come on in. Today is a good day for business. I sent all my workers away, so it's only you, me, and some beautiful women."

Freeway could not believe it. Kurupt was so excited to join forces that he was blind. He had sent away all his workers. This might be easier than he thought it would be.

Kurupt came and put his arm around Freeway and escorted him to the bar, where a fresh glass of rum and Coke was already prepared. Spanish music was playing in the background. Freeway could not believe how excited his cousin was acting, so for a moment, he had no choice but to play along. But he was going to put his plan into action right after he took that first drink with his cousin. He figured since he was going to kill him, he could at least drink with the man one last time.

"I got to admit, Freeway, it was a surprise that you wanted to team up. What changed your mind? And, please, be honest."

"Honestly, I just figure we would be more powerful together," Freeway said while taking a big gulp of his liquor. He wanted to hurry up and get the job done.

"Freeway, it's interesting that you said that because you're aware I keep my ear to the streets."

"So do I."

"No, Freeway, you only deal with people you *want* to deal with."

"That's not true."

"Oh yes, it is. I'm in business with all types of people," Kurupt said while taking the last gulp of his drink.

"So, what you saying? You're better than me?" Freeway asked as he stood up because he was starting to feel dizzy.

"No, Freeway, I'm just a better businessman than you," Kurupt said while pulling out his gun. He could tell that the potent tranquilizer he had laced Freeway's drink was starting to take effect.

Freeway pulled out his gun. He could not believe he had allowed his cousin to bamboozle him. Suddenly, Freeway fell flat on his face. Kurupt picked up Freeway's gun and dragged him over to the sofa, where he had some of his sexy female friends tie him up. Then Kurupt sat on the couch across from him and kept on drinking.

What Freeway didn't know from being so reckless was that Kurupt had always paid good money to know his cousin's *every* move to guarantee that he'd be ready if Freeway ever crossed him. So Kurupt knew Freeway was coming and was well prepared. Moreover, he had released all his workers so it would throw off Freeway, and it did exactly what he wanted it to do.

Kurupt gave his cousin just enough of the tranquilizer to knock him out temporarily. Finally, Kurupt stood over Freeway and poured a bucket of ice-cold water on him to wake him up. Freeway's body almost went into shock when he felt that icy water hit his flesh. He screamed out in confusion, fighting to free himself, but all he managed to do was bang around on the floor. Then Kurupt put his gun to Freeway's head. When Freeway felt the cold steel touch his temple, he stopped moving.

"You know, I should blow your damn brains out right now. What the fuck were you thinking, Freeway?"

"You wouldn't understand."

"Try me."

"It's Belladonna! They got Belladonna."

"Stop being a bitch, Freeway. I told you from day one not to trust that bitch."

"You were always jealous because I got her, and you didn't."

"Are you serious? Listen to yourself. Come on, think about it. She's the sister of Tasha. Don't you think she's grimy?" Kurupt inquired while picking up Freeway and placing him on the couch.

"I watch every move you make, Freeway, because you're a dangerous man, so I have to keep my eye on you."

"If you're going to kill me, just do it."

"I understand that you did not want to come here and do this, but it still gives you no right to turn your back on me, no matter how many disagreements we have."

Freeway just dropped his head in shame. Even though he was drunk off revenge, he knew Kurupt was right. Then Kurupt got off the couch and stuck his gun in Freeway's mouth so deep he choked. Now, Kurupt's whole facial expression changed, and Freeway's heart began to race. For the first time in his life, he felt the fear he had been putting in other people.

"If you were anybody else, I would fucking kill you. You *do* know that, right? I know *exactly* who set you up . . . but I'm not going to tell. I want you to find out on your own and kill them all—*including* Belladonna. If you don't, we are no longer family. Do I make myself clear?"

Freeway nodded as Kurupt pulled the gun from his mouth.

"I'm not giving you any of my money, so I don't know what you're going to tell them, but you better figure out something."

"Just untie me," Freeway growled from the humiliation he felt from being tied up. Kurupt untied him and slowly walked Freeway to the door with the gun pointed at the middle of his back.

"If this ever happens again, I will have no choice but to kill you, Freeway. I hope you understand that."

Freeway turned around, smiled at his cousin, and walked away. Kurupt shook his head. He didn't know why Freeway would smile, knowing he had to feel defeated. He stood at his door, waiting until Freeway was in his car, and drove off. Once he was out of sight, Kurupt felt good that he had finally shown his cousin *he* was the better man.

Freeway drove up the block . . . and parked. He then reached into his duffle bag and pulled out his AR-15 assault rifle, smiling at the thought that Kurupt believed he had defeated him. Freeway knew Kurupt would have some trick up his sleeve. He just didn't know what. Freeway's ego would take joy in killing Kurupt for how he had embarrassed him, but now, his mind could not help but wonder if Belladonna really took part in helping to set him up.

Freeway jumped out of his car and wasted no time returning to his cousin's house to give him the goodbye present of a lifetime. He silently stepped onto the porch and slipped the clip inside his rifle. Kurupt had turned up his music and had begun to party with his lady friends. He didn't realize death stood on his porch, waiting.

Freeway did not waste another second. Instead, he kicked in the door.

Tat, tat, tat.

Freeway shot every female who was dancing beside Kurupt. Kurupt ran to the bar to retrieve his gun, but Freeway hit him in the leg with three quick bullets, the rounds from the assault rifle damn near ripping apart his leg. Then Freeway kicked Kurupt in the face until his whole face was covered in blood, with a broken nose and smashed teeth. Next, Freeway pressed his foot against Kurupt's throat as hard as he could.

"You may be a better businessman, but when it comes to this street shit, *I'm* ruler over all. So how does it feel knowing you're going to die watching me walk out of here with the upper hand . . . as usual?" Kurupt could barely speak. The only thing he could do was spit up blood.

Tat, tat, tat, tat. Freeway ended his cousin's life feeling no remorse. Once that was done, he went through every room until he found all the money. While carrying the cash to his car, his phone began to ring.

Freeway looked all around because he realized the unknown caller had to have been watching him. Every time he finished a job, the guy called right on point. But Freeway saw nobody insight that looked suspicious. So finally, he picked up the phone with anger lacing his voice.

"I'm sick of playing your little fucking game."

"I didn't think you had it in you, Freeway, but you took out your greatest competition. How does it feel to be *that* nigga? Now, here comes the biggest challenge. I want you to kill your father."

Chapter 14

Freeway finally realized what the whole situation was about. It was to end his father's legacy, and the only person who could get close to him was Freeway, but he refused to go through with the deal.

"You got to be kidding me. So, *this* is what it's all about? You want my father's spot?"

"Your father is an OG. I still hear people speaking his name, and I'm sick of it. We are also sick of living in your shadow."

"What the fuck do you mean, 'we'?" Freeway said with an anxious tone because the caller just said more than he was supposed to.

"You know what I mean. The whole city is tired of you running things."

"That's not what you meant. You and somebody else are setting me up."

The caller hung up when he realized that Freeway was getting too clever and was catching on.

Freeway turned, started his car, and sped down the road. He knew precisely who he was going to see next. As he moved through the traffic, he was focused on his game plan . . . until he saw a familiar face. He slowed the car to verify that the young boy was Grizzly.

What in the hell is he doing on this side of town? he thought.

He pulled off to the side of the road without being noticed. The young boy was nervously pacing back and forth and around his car. Then Freeway saw him fidgeting with his phone. It looked as if he was attaching something to a cell phone. A moment later, Grizzly placed the phone to his ear . . . and immediately, Freeway's phone rang.

"What the hell?" Freeway frowned.

He ignored the call and squinted as he watched the boy hang up and redial the number. Then again, his phone rang.

Freeway laughed. "Bingo, you son of a bitch."

Freeway jumped out of the car with his AR-15.

Grizzly realized that Freeway was not answering, so he kept on calling. They were so close to owning New Orleans. He could not let this opportunity slip away.

"You sneaky son of a bitch."

"Freeway, I-I-I can explain."

"Nothing you say can save your ass." Freeway made Grizzly walk to his car, get in, and drive while he sat in the backseat holding the rifle to the back of his head. Freeway could not believe he had let this young buck fool him for so long, but he realized Grizzly was not clever enough to do this alone. He knew there was a mastermind behind this young boy's actions . . . Somebody that had way more pull than Grizzly did.

"Pull over right here."

"Freeway, please, hear me out!"

"Just pull over."

Grizzly knew what happened when Freeway took people into this old, cold, abandoned warehouse. He was probably not going to walk back out alive. As soon as Grizzly opened the car door, Freeway smacked him in the face with the butt of his gun. Then he picked up the boy and threw him headfirst into the driver's-side window. Freeway refrained from doing any more damage because he knew he had to get answers.

"You got some nerve trying to set me up. Have you forgotten who I am?" he asked while pulling the boy out of the window and throwing him on the ground.

He made him crawl to the warehouse, which was also Freeway's execution spot. Everybody knew if Freeway took you there, there was no coming back.

Next, Freeway threw him on the cold floor face-first. Then he kicked him over so he could begin his interrogation. Freeway could not believe that the same young boy he schooled the game to had tried to take him and his family out.

"I'm going to ask you one time . . . Who the fuck are your partners?"

"Freeway, I can't tell you that," Grizzly nervously replied.

Freeway stomped the boy in his stomach repeatedly until he coughed up blood. The boy did not know how much more of Freeway's abuse he could take. Then Freeway took the barrel of his AR-15 and put it against Grizzly's knee. "Let's try this again. Who is working with you? Who is trying to have my whole family set up, and which of you motherfuckers put some hot shit in my girl, Belladonna?"

"Freeway, I can't!"

Tat, tat, tat.

Freeway pulled the trigger, making his AR-15 shells rip red-hot through Grizzly's right kneecap. The bullets wasted no effort in dislocating his knee.

"Aaaah, fuck! OK, OK, I'll tell you!"

"I want the truth. You're young and stupid, but you don't understand that loyalty is more powerful than money. So, I'm giving you a chance to live."

"It was all fake—everything! All of it—the shooting, the hospital pictures of Belladonna—everything was fake. We had a professional makeup artist on hand to make it appear that she had been shot and was covered in blood. Can't you see, Freeway? Belladonna wants you dead, you dumb motherfucker."

"What the fuck are you talking about? And you better not lie," Freeway said while kicking the boy in his face, just in case he thought about lying. The kick in the face would remind him of the pain lying would cost him.

"When your father was doing his thing in the streets, he killed Belladonna and Tasha's father. So she was only with you to get revenge. Tasha never knew this, but Belladonna did. She learned it from ear hustling in the streets."

Freeway went straight into a rage. Just the thought of him being played by a bitch this whole time erupted in his mind like the lava that overflows in an erupting volcano. He immediately put the gun to Grizzly's head.

"I swear to God, if you are lying to me, you will *never* see daylight again—do you hear me?" he roared.

"I'm not lying, Freeway. This is real facts. I can prove it."

"How?"

"I can reveal to you who else is behind this whole assault on your life."

"Who is it?" Freeway said in an anxious voice. He was ready to know who else put a tag on his life.

"Lazarus."

"What?" Freeway shouted as he hit Grizzly repeatedly in the stomach with the butt of his gun.

"You're lying!" he growled with each strike.

"Stop, stop! I'm telling you the truth. Lazarus is tired of living in your shadows. Think about it, Freeway. He set you up to go to your cousin's house. Why do you think he was pulled, unable to accompany you? He orchestrated all of this."

When Freeway thought about it, he recalled that Lazarus was ready for everything they had gone through. He already had his gun in the car, and Lazarus used to hint around all the time about how much he wanted to rob and take over the Gambino brothers' empire.

"What about this bitch, Brenda? What is she in this for?"

"She's just in it for the money. She doesn't give a fuck about you, me, Belladonna, or Tasha. She just wanted the money. But that's not the big shock of this whole situation, Freeway."

"You mean there's more? What can be more shocking than all of this?"

"Lazarus is Belladonna's oldest brother."

The news caught Freeway so badly off guard that he dropped his gun. He realized he was getting played the entire time. He wondered how he could have been so stupid. He grew up with this nigga and kept him safe too when everybody else wanted to rob and kill him because he was a snake. This hurt Freeway's heart to know that the nigga he had trusted was indeed the snake that everybody claimed he was.

Then Freeway picked up his gun. Something was wrong! Grizzly *had* to be lying.

"That's impossible! Lazarus was from Shreveport, and Tasha could not stand his ass," Freeway said while pointing the gun back in Grizzly's face, smiling because he thought he had caught Grizzly in a lie.

"Freeway, come on—think. They all had different fathers, but Belladonna and Lazarus had the *same* father. Once Belladonna told Lazarus who your father was three years ago, *that's* when the plan kicked in."

"You've got one chance to live—if you help me set him up. If so, I'll let you walk away."

"What other choice do I have? I'm down."

Hannibal sat behind his desk at his car dealership with his mind all over the place. From a phone call he had just received, he knew this day was coming, but he hoped it would never have to come down to this. Then his fiancée, Sukie, walked through the door. She knew him better than anybody. She stopped in her tracks and asked him what was wrong.

"Nothing," he answered.

"Hannibal, don't do that. You know I know you, so what's wrong?"

"It's my son."

"Oh, how's he doing? You two need to stop worrying about what people say and see each other."

"He's coming to kill me. He finally wants the name."

"What a minute. Freeway promised you he would never come for your throne, so what gives?"

"It doesn't matter. I've been preparing for this day for ten years. He has earned it, but I just can't let him think he can walk in here and kill me over the legacy I built for all of us."

Sukie was a Spanish chick who did not play games when it came down to Hannibal. So she headed to the file cabinet, pulled out a 9 mm, cocked it back, and headed for the door.

"Babe, where the hell are you going?"

"Your son wants a war? Let's go win ourselves a war."

"Babe, calm down. We need to think this through. You know I'm not in the streets anymore, and I at least want to give my son the benefit of the doubt."

"Hannibal, are you serious right now? This little nigga wants to kill you and take over the throne that you have—and you want to sit there and *think* this out? Stop being a bitch."

Hannibal jumped up in a blink of an eye and slammed his fiancée's face on the desk. Sukie started to smile because this was the old Hannibal she was looking for. But her smile was quickly erased when he snatched the gun out of her hand and put it to the back of her head. She realized that she had pushed the demon out of him that she thought he had buried.

"Don't forget who the fuck you talking to, bitch. War or no war, at the end of the day, that's *still* my son. So if I said we need to think this out, that's *exactly* what we're going to do."

He released Sukie, removed the clip from the gun, and threw the 9 mm on the desk. Then he sat back in his chair, realizing the demon in him had never left. It was just on a break. Hannibal could not understand why Freeway's right-hand man, Lazarus, would sell Freeway out, disclosing the information that his son was coming for his throne. Sukie was about to explain herself when her apology was interrupted by a knock on the door. Hannibal did not feel like being bothered, so he shouted, "Go away."

"What do you mean, go away? I got the numbers for today."

"I said, go away, or else."

"Or else what, nigga? Stop playing and open this door."

Sukie looked at Hannibal and knew precisely how he was feeling. But unfortunately, the people at the car dealership he hired did not know how dangerous he was. They didn't realize that he was once the most feared man in New Orleans.

The guy walked into Hannibal's office anyway.

"Look, Mr. Moore, I need you to sign these papers. I don't have all day. I'm trying to go home."

Sukie walked out of the room and locked the door behind her. She knew what was about to go down.

"Sir, can you hurry up? Come on, boss man," the guy said while snapping his fingers in Hannibal's face.

Hannibal picked up the 9 mm from the desk. He put the clip in, and the guy threw up his hands, but it was too late. Hannibal stood to his feet.

Pow, pow, pow.

Hannibal shot the guy in the head three times. After firing that gun, he knew he had no choice but to go to war with his son. And he secretly doubted he could defeat him.

Chapter 15

Freeway sat in his car across from the hospital and watched Brenda get into her vehicle and pull off. He followed her. She had no idea she was about to be the next victim on the great Freeway's list. She pulled up in a driveway of a house that looked very nice . . . a little too nice for it to be on a nurse's salary.

Freeway popped his glove compartment and pulled out his Glock. He was going to murder this bitch with no questions asked. Brenda walked into the house without a care in the world.

Freeway thought to himself, *The nerve of this bitch to act so calmly*. But all of that was about to end. He got out of the car and headed to Brenda's three-story home.

He walked to the window and peeked inside but could not see any movement there. Then he went around to the side of the house where the kitchen window appeared. He peered through that window but again saw nobody was there. *There is no way she's in this big house by herself*, he thought.

Then he went around the back and quietly made his way up the steps that led to the deck. The glass door was halfway cracked, and the grill on the deck was smoking, giving off the delicious smell of barbeque ribs and burgers. That's why there was no movement inside the house because whoever was with her was about to have a cookout. But all that was about to come to an end . . . and so were their lives.

Freeway stood on the steps as he heard voices and footsteps coming from the deck. He could tell that they were near the grill by the distance of their voices, so he peeked to see who Brenda was talking to.

"What the fuck," Freeway said, surprised to see a white man standing at the grill.

At first, Freeway thought it was a cop, but he figured Brenda was not that stupid to date a cop while doing the mess she was involved in.

"Mommy, Mommy," a little girl said, running to Brenda.

"Shit." Freeway let out a sigh, wishing a kid was not involved. But this was not going to stop him from handling his business. Freeway cocked his gun, then ran onto the deck.

"Put your fucking hands in the air!"

"Freeway, what the hell are you doing here?" Brenda said as she dropped her plate. Freeway watched the plate smash to the deck with a smile on his face. The white man was terrified. He had no clue what was going on.

"I have five thousand in the safe in the bedroom, but that's all I have—not a penny more," the man said.

"He's not here for the money, honey," Brenda said, stepping in front of her husband so Freeway would not target him.

"Well, let me find out you like white men. Guess you the type to say niggas ain't shit, huh?" Freeway said with a sick smile on his face. The little girl was holding her mom's leg, scared to death.

"Freeway, you know you can't touch me, so what's the use of doing all this?" Brenda asked.

Freeway ran over and smacked Brenda in the face with his pistol. She hit the deck while grabbing her face. Blood rapidly seeped through her fingers.

"Bitch, I already know all of you are setting me up. You, Lazarus, and Belladonna. You got me, but it's time to pay the price now. Where the fuck is Belladonna? Don't fucking lie to me."

"I don't know, Freeway. I just take the phone calls and tell you where to go."

Freeway grabbed her husband and put the gun to his head.

"I'm going to ask you one more time."

"You wasting your time, Freeway. I know nothing."

Freeway released her husband. He had a better idea of getting the information he wanted. He pushed Brenda out of the way, then grabbed her daughter. Brenda's whole expression and reaction changed instantly. Freeway now knew he had her right where he wanted her.

"Freeway, no. Please, I'll tell you what you want to know. But please, please, don't hurt my little girl."

"Where the fuck is Belladonna?" he asked while holding the little girl with the gun to her head.

"Please, just put her down. I got all the information you need."

"You don't run shit. Your time of giving orders has passed. Now, where the fuck is she?"

Pow, pow.

Freeway switched directions and shot her husband in the throat and chest. Brenda dropped to her knees. She knew Freeway was not playing.

"Oh, I'm sorry. Did I break your concentration? You better start talking, or the next bullet is going inside this little bitch's head."

"She's with Lazarus. She's with Lazarus. Please, Freeway, let my daughter go."

"How did it feel thinking you had defeated me and were on top? You knew who I was and what I was about. You were a fool to allow yourself to think you would live to tell your story. I'm not going to kill your daughter because I am not that coldhearted."

Brenda started to feel relieved, but that emotion would be short-lived. Freeway took out another gun and removed the clip but kept one bullet in the chamber. He threw the weapon near Brenda's feet, and while still pointing his gun at her, he told her to grab it.

"Pick it up. You got ten seconds to shoot yourself in the head—or I'll kill your daughter."

"What? Come on, Freeway. I'm innocent in all of this."

"Ten, nine, eight, seven . . ."

"Freeway, please."

"Six, five, four, three . . ."

"I love you, baby girl," Brenda said while putting the gun in her mouth and closing her eyes with tears flowing down her face. Freeway looked at her and smiled, feeling no remorse whatsoever.

Pow. Brenda's brains flew everywhere. Her daughter screamed as she watched her mom's lifeless body drop like a rotten apple from a tree. Freeway pulled out his phone and called someone to come and pick up the little girl.

After waiting for two hours, someone picked up the little girl. Good money was paid to ensure his connect took her to a good home. Then Freeway headed back to the abandoned building where he still had Grizzly tied up. He no longer needed Grizzly and was going to end that loose end as soon as he reached the building. He slowed down at the light when he saw Sukie walking into a corner store, so he decided to go in and say hi and ask how his father was doing.

Freeway noticed her bodyguard was with her, and he wondered if his father knew he was supposed to kill him. So he decided to go and tell Sukie it was all a lie, and he was getting framed before his father got the wrong idea, and they went to war for no reason.

Freeway pulled into the parking lot as Sukie walked outside. She froze in her tracks as Freeway got out of his car. He waved at her, but all her eyes were focused on was the gun he had tucked in his waistband beneath his belt. Finally, she yelled out to her bodyguard.

"That's him! Shoot, shoot," she screamed as she ducked behind her other bodyguard, who came out of the store right behind her. She pushed him forward so she could hide behind him while he took out Freeway. The other bodyguard jumped out of the car immediately.

Pow, pow, pow.

Freeway ducked behind his vehicle and could not believe the mess he had just walked into. Both bodyguards were now shooting at him.

Tink, tink. The bullets were hitting his car, and a couple of shots shattered the glass as Freeway climbed back inside his vehicle and grabbed his AR-15.

Tat, tat, tat.

Their little handguns did not stand a chance against his assault rifle. They dropped their guns immediately, but that did not stop Freeway. He repeatedly shot the first bodyguard in his chest until the bullets lifted his whole body off the ground and finally sent him crashing into the car behind him. Then he walked over to Sukie and made her get on the ground.

"You might want to close your eyes for this one, bitch," Freeway said while pulling the trigger and sending multiple bullets into the other bodyguard's face, making his head pop and brains splatter all over Sukie.

Sukie knew and heard of the stories about Freeway but had never experienced or had been in his presence. She saw why her man feared the day that he'd have to go to war with his son. She saw that Freeway was way more dangerous than Hannibal.

"Get your ass in the car and hurry the fuck up," Freeway ordered.

Sukie wasted no time in following Freeway's orders. Once they were in the truck, Freeway made her call Hannibal. She was so scared that she could barely dial the number. Hannibal answered but was not happy to hear his son's voice come over her phone.

"I see you got your bitch out here making niggas shoot at me," Freeway said.

"You don't want this war, son."

"There is no war. I been set up."

"I don't give a fuck what you say, and I don't believe you. One of us is going to die today."

"You're a fucking idiot. Did you forget I got your bitch right here?"

"See, unlike you, I don't let a bitch control my life. That's how *you* got in this position in the first place. I only used her to stay out of the limelight. You can kill that bitch as far as I care." Before Hannibal had a chance to hang up, he heard two gunshots and knew Freeway had just killed Sukie without question, but he did not have any feelings for her. Frustrated, Hannibal threw the phone on his desk.

He looked at his main hit man, who sat across from him in his office.

"I need you to go handle this job. My son is not letting up, and he's coming. He just killed Sukie."

"Are you sure there will be no hard feelings when I kill him?" the man asked.

"If you kill him, there will be no hard feelings. My son is no average street nigga, though. He will try to kill you on sight."

"Hannibal, no disrespect, but have you forgotten how long I've been doing this?"

"Let me remind you about the job last year when you had to kill that bitch. My son just shot a bitch without hesitation to prove a point, so what the hell do you think he'll do to you? Get the fuck out of my office and go handle this shit right now."

"Do you know where I can find him?"

"He's probably at the warehouse now, so go."

After the hit man left, Hannibal knew he would have to strap up. He also knew that his hit man did not stand a chance against the son who shared the same blood as him, but no matter what it took, he would not lose his throne to his son.

Chapter 16

Freeway walked inside the warehouse holding his Glock. Grizzly could see the look in Freeway's eyes and knew that he had been out there putting the murder game down. He was feeling relieved because he knew now he would be released.

"Where the fuck is Lazarus hiding? I know he would not be stupid enough to be at his own crib." Freeway said while pointing the Glock straight at Grizzly's head.

"Freeway, why are you still pointing the gun at me? I thought we was past this, and I need a doctor, man, bad, please."

"Where the fuck is Lazarus's hideout spot?"

"I'm not answering another question until you take me to the hospital," Grizzly said, hoping Freeway would take the bait that he needed him.

Freeway let off a bullet and shot Grizzly in his other leg. "Does it look like I'm playing with you?"

"OK, I'll take you to his hideout," screamed Grizzly in pain. "Just help me out of these ropes you put me in."

"Oh, you will *not* be going anywhere with me. Tell me, or I'll change my mind about letting you live. I can always ask Brenda and let her live instead of you."

Grizzly hurried up and spat out the address because he wanted to be the one to live instead of Brenda, but he had no idea he was being played.

"I appreciate it, Grizzly. I appreciate you playing the game because the game just played you," Freeway said while unloading four bullets into Grizzly's chest, causing his body to flip out of the chair. Then Freeway got on the phone and called his cleanup man to come and pick up the body. After that, he exited the warehouse and proceeded to the address Grizzly had delivered to him moments before the bullets met with his chest.

Grizzly and Brenda knew the type of man they were dealing with, but they thought their plan with Belladonna was so clever that they would not get caught. They even fooled Tasha into making her believe Belladonna had really been shot. They fooled everybody just to get a massive piece of the pie, of the good life that New Orleans had to offer. But it cost them all their lives, and it was only about to get worse because Freeway would serve everybody a cold dish of revenge.

Freeway stopped at all his cash houses and hideout spots, making everybody shut down shop. Then after he handled his business with Lazarus and Belladonna and killed his father, he would leave New Orleans.

He arrived at his last stash house and paid off everybody that worked for him. Then he told them that there would be no more business. He was wrapping it up for good once he finished the task he had to do.

His workers were shocked. They could not believe that Freeway was calling it quits. They knew how much he loved power and money. However, Freeway did not break down any details. He merely told them it was his time to step out of the game.

As he was putting money into his trunk, he heard gunshots from a distance, and his workers screamed for him to duck.

Tat, tat, tat, tat. Freeway recognized those sounds. They were bullets from an assault rifle whistling in his direction. He tried to duck behind his car, but it was catching incredible damage. Freeway quickly grabbed his AR-15 and went to return fire . . . but to his surprise, he saw nobody wherever he looked.

More bullets flew his way when he looked at the house across the street. He tried to run back to the car, but the shots were coming rapidly, causing him to return to his stash house. Once inside, he ran upstairs, made a hard right, and slid into the first bedroom. Quickly, he closed the door and flipped the bed over to barricade it. Then he looked out the window to try to locate the shooter.

"Son of a bitch. So you sent your hit man after me, huh, pops?" Freeway said as he spotted the gunman in the house across the street in a bedroom.

Freeway kicked out the window and aimed his gun outside. He had the gunman in his scope and began firing. The gunman took several hits, and Freeway quickly ran out of the house to finish the job. He saw the hit man staggering from the house, holding his bleeding shoulder.

Tat, tat, tat.

Freeway hit him with more bullets to his legs. The hit man had no choice but to drop to the ground as his gun fell too. Freeway slowly walked over and kicked his body over. The gunman began coughing up blood and talking in a weak but defeated voice.

"Your father said you would not be an easy target, and you would kill with no hesitation. A job well done. I have never been shot before."

"Not only did you get shot, but you will also die today."

"Do you think you can really defeat your father? He built his life on not giving a fuck."

"I can, and I will, but one thing's for sure. You will not be here to witness any of this," Freeway said with a sadistic smile as he sent multiple bullets to the hit man's chest. He watched him take his last breath, then laughed about it.

Finished there, Freeway jumped into his car and drove back to the projects to switch to one of his better cars. Unfortunately, the one he was driving had taken too many bullets, which would draw the attention of the police.

He switched cars and paid somebody to burn his old car. If there was one thing he was good at, it was covering up his tracks. He never did a half-assed job and never left a job unfinished. He knew his father was ruthless, but he had the best weapon to defeat him.

While riding down the road, Freeway thought it was funny how this war had nothing to do with his father, but now because he allowed outsiders to get inside his head, Freeway had no choice but to kill him.

Freeway pulled up to the address Grizzly gave him. It was a nice, everyday Sunday house with a fence. It was something that you bought when you were ready to settle down with the love of your life. Freeway rolled down his window and got the shock of his life. Lazarus and Belladonna were on the porch—kissing.

Suddenly, it hit Freeway. They were not brother and sister—they were lovers. They had fooled everybody, even Tasha. For a brief moment, he felt bad about killing Tasha. She was a victim in this too. Belladonna knew the attitude he had and knew eventually, he would kill Tasha. Finally,

Freeway figured out that Belladonna was not the innocent girl he thought she was. He rolled up his window and could not believe how he had been played, but he was about to get to the bottom of this. He drove up the block and walked back down to scope out his surroundings. He did not want to feel like he was closed in. Soon, Lazarus and Belladonna walked back into the home.

Lazarus called Grizzly, and Belladonna called Brenda. They were both starting to worry when neither of the workers picked up. Then Lazarus got off the couch and started pacing. Belladonna began tapping her foot. She was getting apprehensive now.

She jumped up after the sixth time she called and got no answer. She was the first to break the silence and address the elephant in the room.

"What if Freeway figured it out? What'll we do?"

"Baby, calm down. Trust me, Freeway may be good at what he does, but he is not *that* damn good. We got this."

"No, no, I don't trust this. Suddenly, nobody is answering their phone?"

"Chill out and calm down."

"How can you be so calm? Do you *know* what Freeway will do to us?"

"You're overacting. Just calm your nerves," Lazarus said while kissing Belladonna on the forehead and helping her back to the couch.

Freeway kept seeing the same number calling the phone he took from Grizzly, so he called back the number.

"See, baby, look. Grizzly's calling me right now."

"Well, answer it," Belladonna said excitedly.

"Hello?"

"You dirty son of a bitch. I trusted you."

"Freeway, is that you?"

"You know exactly who the fuck it is, and when I find you, I'm going to kill you, but first, I'm going to make you watch me kill Belladonna right in front of your face. By the way, good job on making me and my father go to war, but that's good as handled too."

"Freeway, Freeway—"

"You said he would *not* find out. What did he say?" Belladonna asked, feeling scared for her life.

"Get your shit. We got to get the hell out of here."

As soon as Belladonna was about to run to the back to gather her things, Freeway kicked in the door, smacked Lazarus with his pistol, then shot Belladonna in the back of the leg. He dragged her from the hallway and threw her on the couch. Just looking at her pissed off Freeway, so he smacked her with his pistol too. Lazarus wasted no time in begging for his life. Freeway thought, the nerve of this nigga.

Freeway demanded that Lazarus stand, and while grabbing Lazarus around his neck, he kicked Belladonna in her stomach.

"Open your eyes, bitch. *You* did this. You wanted to play me, but now, you wanna cry like *you're* the victim," Freeway said while gripping his arms tighter around Lazarus's neck with his gun pointed dead at his temple.

Next, he threw Lazarus on the couch and shot him in both knees so he could not run. Then he grabbed Belladonna in the same choke-hold position he had Lazarus in. Belladonna quickly began to express why she did what she did.

"You and your father aren't shit. You will rot in hell, Freeway."

"Not before you. You had the nerve to punish me and set me up for a murder my father committed when he was in the streets."

"Wait, Freeway, you love me, baby."

Freeway pushed her onto the couch and looked at the woman that he once would have fought the world for. He smiled at her, and she smiled back.

Pow, pow, pow.

Freeway put as many bullets into her chest as he could. After that, he pulled out a brand-new clip, slid it into his gun, and pointed it at Lazarus. He immediately shot Lazarus in both arms and twice more in his legs.

"I'm not going to kill you with bullets, Lazarus. Oh no, what you did to me, you deserve to burn in hell." Freeway quickly went to his car, got the gasoline can, and poured it all over the house. The remainder of it he poured onto Lazarus.

"Wait, Freeway. I'll give you the money from the Italian brothers we killed."

"No, you keep it. You may need to buy a good seat in hell."

Freeway stepped outside, lit a match, and threw it into the house. Instantly, the place went up in flames. On his way to his car, he heard Lazarus screaming. Freeway walked away with a satisfied smile on his face.

"You're next, pops."

Chapter 17

Freeway had taken a picture of the hit man when he killed him. He sent the photo to his father and waited for the phone to ring. This war with his father was not going to be easy. His father was never there for him after his mother died in a car accident. Freeway remembered the day his father left him at his grandmother's house when he was 15 like it was just yesterday.

Hannibal pulled up to his mother's house with his son, Freeway, in the passenger seat, looking happy to spend time with his father. Hannibal cut the car off and waved at his mother, but she did not wave back because she knew what he was about to do.

"Look, little man, I love having you with me."

"I love you too, Father."

"But what I do for a living, I can't have you around me all the time."

"Sure, you can, Father. You're just a construction worker."

"Son, it's deeper than that. I only do that to cover up what I really do, and I have not done construction for over four years. I only told you that so you would not worry."

"So, what do you do for a living?"

"You honestly don't know what I do for a living?"

"Come on, pops, what is this, a game or something? I know you sell drugs," Freeway said very nervously to him. His father always seemed angry.

"I don't want you ever to open your mouth and tell your little friends what I do for a living. Do you understand?"

"Why not? What you do is cool."

Slap. Hannibal slapped his son's face.

Freeway balled up, hoping his father would not hit him again. This is why Freeway feared having conversations with his father. He knew how his father never seemed to be happy.

"That's why I'm leaving you at your grandmother's house. You're too green in these streets. Get the fuck out of my car."

"But, Father—"

"Get the fuck out and don't come back until you grow the fuck up."

"But, Father, I don't want to leave."

Hannibal jumped out of his car, snatched his son from the vehicle, and threw him to the ground. Freeway could not believe his father treated him this way.

"Look at you! You look sad and sorry. You don't have the heart to ride with me in the streets."

"I hate you!" Freeway said while getting up and running to his grandmother's house. Hannibal got into his car, but his mother stopped him by standing in front of it. She motioned for Hannibal to roll down his window. So he did but with an attitude.

"Ma, what do you want? I got things I'm trying to do."

"What's wrong with you? Why do you treat your son this way?"

"Because he's weak, that's why."

"You know, one day, Hannibal, that boy is going to be the death of you."

"The boy has to grow some balls first," he said with laughter in the back of his throat.

Hannibal pulled out of the driveway, never to see his son again until years later.

Freeway clenched his teeth when he came out of daydreaming about how his father had turned his back on him when he was a teenager. His father was why Freeway hated people and had trust issues all his life, but Freeway began to smile when he thought about the day his father ran into him, and he was the big baller on the block.

Knock, knock.

"Who is it?"

"Hannibal."

The guy opened the door to Hannibal. Even though Hannibal was out of the game, he still had power and did not like how the money he controlled was being messed with.

"Who the fuck told you fools to run up on my turf? There are rules to this shit."

"Hannibal, listen, that shit is out of my control. I just run numbers here."

"Look, I know you fools ran on my turf because the boy I shot said he got the package from this stash house," Hannibal said while pulling out his gun and cocking it.

"Yo, Freeway, come out here. We got a problem."

"Yeah, call your punk-ass boss up here so I can tell him who I am."

Hannibal paced back and forth, waiting for whoever's ass came out and confronted him, but, oh boy, was he surprised to see that the top dog was no other than his son. "What the fuck are you doing here?" barked Hannibal.

"No, the question is, what the fuck are you doing here raising hell inside my organization, popping off at your mouth? This shit is no longer yours. I run this shit now," frowned Freeway.

"I tell you what. I'm happy you finally got some balls and became a man. But let's get one thing straight. The streets will never be yours as long as I still have the throne. You're the prince, and I'm the king," smirked Hannibal.

"I tell you what, Father. You can keep this shit because I want you to know the only reason you have your throne is that I allow it," laughed Freeway.

"Ha-ha. Well, look at junior running things."

"I think you may want to take a look around, old man, because ain't no juniors in this bitch," Freeway said while pulling out his gun.

Hannibal slowly backed away, telling Freeway that he could run the streets for the moment, but he vowed they would collide again one day. Hannibal left that trap house knowing his son truly was in charge, and he wondered if he could defeat him if they ever really went to war.

Ring, ring.

The phone ringing broke Freeway from thinking about how he had made his father stand down. He picked up the phone to an angry Hannibal.

"You think you can defeat me? You bring your ass on if you think you got what it takes to take my throne."

"You brought this on yourself. You chose to believe other people and let them fools poison your mind, but now, it's too late. So today, you die by *my* hand."

"Freeway, you have *never* been my son. You were too weak and a fucking embarrassment."

"You mean the same way you were weak when you walked out of my trap house defeated," Freeway said with a laugh to follow up.

"You come here, Freeway, and you will die."

"If I go there, Hannibal, *you'll* die."

"I'll be waiting for you," Hannibal said, slamming down the phone.

Hannibal had to admit he did feel a slight fear of his son. This was not the same little boy he smacked around as a teenager. Hannibal made all his workers leave. He knew his son was coming. He could hear it in his voice. Then he sat at his desk cleaning his 9 mm. He was going to kill his son by any means necessary.

Freeway knew he had to be careful because, truth be told, his father still held power, and he was not going to let it go or give it up lightly. So now, Freeway pulled off, heading to his father's dealership. He knew today was the day he would bring his A game, or it would be the day he took his last breath.

Freeway pulled up to the dealership. Everything was pitch black.

He popped his trunk and smiled when he pulled out his gun. He walked away from his car, leaving his trunk open as he made his way through all the vehicles in the parking lot and let off two rounds.

Pow, pow. "Come on, Hannibal, come out and face the music."

Hannibal sat at his desk drinking liquor. He would move when he wanted to. "I advise you to come out here right now, or I'll start shooting every last one of these cars in your lot," Freeway yelled.

Finally, Hannibal put the clip into his gun and cocked it back as he heard Freeway shooting the glass out of many of his cars, yelling, "I own the lot."

He had to laugh because now he finally saw his son was just like him, but unfortunately, it was too late.

He got up and opened the door. He had a clear shot at Freeway, and Freeway never even saw him.

Pow, pow. Freeway took a bullet in the shoulder, sending his gun flying out of his hand. Hannibal did not know it would be this easy. He had heard in the streets how Freeway was a mastermind at killing, but he wasn't afraid because he did not see what the talk was about.

Hannibal walked up to Freeway and put the gun to his head.

"You are nothing, Freeway. The streets say you are a genius at getting your kill. Well, right now, I can't tell. Look at who's on top and always will be on top."

Freeway started to laugh.

"Look at you. You're defeated, and you got the nerve to laugh?"

"Because you're the fool. I'm the mastermind. I knew if you got a shot off on me instead of killing me, your ego would have to get in the last word. Well, now, it's *my* turn. Get him, girl!"

Pow, pow, pow, pow. Hannibal's body flew back from four bullets catching him in the chest. Freeway stood up. Hannibal lay there holding his chest, bleeding out, but the pain got worse when he saw Sukie walk up to him with a gun in her hand. "See, I spared her life because you wanted her dead, and I knew the anger she has for you would become useful. I know what you're thinking. You thought I killed her. But see, that's where that mastermind kicked in. I only held the gun near the phone and shot it."

"You stupid son of a bitch. I had your back since day one, but *you* are the one that's not loyal," Sukie said while repeatedly kicking Hannibal in the face.

"Hold up, baby girl. I don't want him to die like this. I want him to burn in hell," Freeway said while pulling Sukie back to prevent her from kicking him any longer.

Freeway went to his car and pulled out four gas cans. He poured some on many of the vehicles. Then he dragged Hannibal back inside his office. Sukie poured gas all over Hannibal's desk. Finally, Freeway picked up his father and slammed him on the desk headfirst.

"Check his pockets," Freeway ordered.

Sukie bent over to search his pockets, and Freeway pulled out his gun and stuck it to the back of her head.

"Did you forget that you tried to kill me, bitch?"

"But, Freeway, I just helped you take down your father!"

"Didn't you just hear him call me the mastermind? You were just a pawn in the mix."

Sukie tried her best to tell Freeway how much she could be helpful to him, but Freeway was not buying one bit. "Bitch, I'm out of the game, and you're out of pocket."

Pow. Freeway shot her in the back of the head. Her dead weight fell over Hannibal. Then he poured gasoline on both of their bodies.

"Son, is it too late to tell you I love you? You own the throne now."

"Correction, I *always* owned the throne. I just let you hold it down," Freeway said while lighting a match and throwing it on his father's body.

Whoosh.

The bodies instantly caught fire. Freeway quickly left the building and New Orleans. He needed to regroup.

Chapter 18

Naomi

Atlanta, Georgia

The beeping of the monitors awoke Naomi from her deep slumber. Sleep had evaded her for over a week since the moment that she had received the news that Calista's baby daddy had been killed, and she had a strong feeling that Calista's father had a hand in it. Unfortunately, she was also facing her own demise, which sent her emotions and anxieties into overdrive.

Different parts of her life flashed before her eyes, and her brain was streaming them. The drug abuse, the physical abuse from men to feed her crack habit . . . The abandonment issues that she caused Calista, who, at times, raised herself. Naomi felt that her cancer diagnosis was her Karma for all the bad decisions she allowed to fill her life.

The word "cancer" bounced around in her head as she lay in bed at Harbor Grace Hospice Center. Her mind reflected on all the mistakes she had made in life. Her biggest one was keeping Calista from her father. She knew her days were numbered as cancer took a portion of her life daily. She prayed about it, to no resolve.

Freeway had always provided for her and Calista, even though he wasn't prominent in her life. Calista was Naomi's only child, and she felt Freeway's lifestyle wasn't conducive to raising a child. Plus, they weren't in love or a couple when she was conceived. They both belonged to the streets. He ruled them, and she couldn't stay out of them.

Now, twenty-plus years later, she needed him. She knew she was a breath away from death's door and didn't want to leave Calista without knowing her father. She had hesitated to contact Freeway, but she needed to call him.

She dialed the number, then sighed. "Lawd, please fix this."

The seconds between every ring seemed like hours.

"Hello," answered Freeway.

"Hey, Cal, I'm bad off. I need you to step up with our daughter," a winded Naomi informed him.

Her words were met with silence and light breathing on the other end.

"I always prayed to hear those words . . . years ago. But I haven't heard that name in ages. So, why now?" he pried.

"I have cancer, and I'm knocking on heaven's door," she responded.

"Our baby is in Memphis, as you know. I need to see her," she pleaded. "I really need you and her to forgive me."

"I have no heaven or hell to put you in. As far as forgiveness, I did that years ago," he responded. "We both made mistakes in our lives."

Naomi was relieved and impressed by how much Freeway had grown mentally. "I wanted to hate you for shutting me out after I learned Calista was my daughter. But Karma and God did that. I have always had a love for you being my daughter's mother, so that overrode any resentment I had for your actions. I always understood your decision, just never agreed with it," he responded.

"Thank you, Cal," mumbled Naomi as she ended the call.

Freeway heard someone talking in the background, whom he assumed was a nurse. His thoughts were interrupted by his driver.

"Hey, boss, you good?" questioned the driver.

Freeway stared off dolefully and replied, "We're headed back to Memphis." Freeway sighed as he ran his hand over his face. The one moment he prayed for was now the moment he was regretting.

"I'm on it, boss," responded his driver.

Freeway had always been remorseful for never telling Naomi how he had really felt about her.

"Thank you," Freeway sighed.

Calista & Freeway

Memphis, Tennessee

"Calista, I know you were just young and in love." But no matter the choice her daughter made, Naomi still loved her.

"Well, Ma, I have nothing left here, so I'm ready to come and join you."

"I'm glad to hear it. However, there's one thing you must do first."

"Anything for you, Mom. What is it?" asked an excited Calista.

"There's somebody you must meet. That person is waiting for you at the coffee shop a couple of blocks away from your church."

"Is this a joke?" Calista asked.

"No, it's not, and you don't have to walk. Instead, a ride should be coming for you that he's sending."

As Calista listened to her mom, she noticed a black Suburban truck pull up. The truck was nice and sleek, which caused her to assume that the ride couldn't be for her. Then a guy got out of it wearing an all-black suit and proceeded to walk in her direction.

"Mom, let me call you back."

"OK, honey." Naomi hung up, figuring that Calista's ride must have arrived.

Calista grabbed Amari, not knowing who the guy was walking up to them, and she was very cautious regarding her daughter. They had been through so much already. She didn't want to have more trouble.

As the guy got closer, she became anxious. She couldn't lie. He was handsome. If her mom knew about this, she felt she couldn't be in any danger.

"Are you Calista?"

"Yes, I am." Calista felt a lump in her throat as if her words were getting lost before they rolled off her tongue.

"Please, follow me. My boss is waiting to meet you," the man told her.

"Wait a minute. Who's your boss?" she questioned.

"I hate being rude, but we don't have all day. My boss isn't the type of man you should keep waiting."

"I understand, but I don't know you," she retorted.

"Your name is Calista, right?"

"Yes."

"Well, Calista, please come with me. I assure you that you are not in any danger," he replied, not elaborating further about his boss's identity.

Calista slowly rose. She was curious about who his boss was. Her mind was racing. She had no clue who he was.

The guy opened the door for her when she got to the truck. After she was securely inside, he slammed the door, which startled her. They drove for about ten minutes until they arrived at the coffee shop. The handsome driver got out and opened the door for her once more.

While she held her daughter tightly, the man escorted them into the coffee shop. They stopped at the third table. When she saw the man at the table, she couldn't believe her eyes. She looked just like him. He stood up out of respect, and the words he said almost made her faint.

"Naomi told me about her condition and asked me to be here for you," he said. "Calista, hi. I'm your father."

"This has to be a joke. My father died when I was young," she argued as her knees began to weaken hearing this news.

"May I?" He reached out to take Amari.

"I don't let anybody hold her." But to her surprise, Amari went right to him.

"Why the hell is she so comfortable with you? She normally shies away from strangers."

"To be honest, for the last two years, I've been stopping by the day care she used to go to."

"Does my mom know you're here?"

"Of course, she does. It was her idea that we finally meet."

"I don't mean to be rude, but what is your name?" Calista asked.

"Freeway or Cal. Most know me by Freeway," he smirked.

"That makes sense. I guess Mom named me after you."

"Yes, you were. I need you to know that I have always supported you all financially. But it was your mom's idea that I not be active in your life," he explained.

"Why now? Why do you want to meet me now?"

"As I told you, this was your mother's idea. I heard about her battling cancer, and she wants me to be here for you." Freeway kept rocking his granddaughter.

"So, you still could care less about us?"

"That's not true at all. It's all on your mother."

"Yeah, right. You're just another deadbeat father. Give me my damn baby."

"Listen to me. You need to hear me out, and I mean listen *really* well."

"Why the fuck do I need to listen to you, dead-beat?" Calista sneered angrily. She was infuriated at his presence.

"I understand you're angry, but I have my reasons, baby girl."

"I got beat on and mistreated by so many men. Where were *you* when I needed you?" Calista got up to walk away.

"Who do you think killed your baby daddy? That motherfucker had to die. Nobody fucks with what's mine," Freeway growled.

Calista stopped in her tracks when she heard her father admit to killing the man that had caused her so much pain. She turned around and looked at her father with tears rolling down her face.

"I spared him for too long. You're my daughter, and I fucking love you. *That's* why I stepped out of the shadows and killed that bastard," he added.

"I hate you for not being there."

"I know you do, but leaving you and your mother was the only way I could keep you safe. You need to understand that," he explained.

"Keep me safe from what? Who the fuck are you?"

"Let's just say my name is well known in the streets," he told her.

"I'm sorry, but that answer just isn't good enough."

Calista needed more information than what her father was giving her.

"You're definitely my daughter." Freeway smiled at how demanding and consistent his daughter was.

"If you're my father, I need answers, and I need them *now*." Calista banged her fist on the table out of anger and frustration.

"Trust me, baby girl, the less you know about me, the better." He wanted to tell his daughter so much, but he knew he couldn't.

"So, are you planning on being in my life full time?"

"Not exactly," he admitted.

"What the fuck . . ."

"I know how it sounds, but trust me. It's for your safety."

"Just tell me who you are, at least. I deserve that much."

"I'm your father," he answered smugly.

"Don't play me for stupid. You know what I mean."

"I've done a lot of shit in these streets. And since you're my daughter, people could use you against me as leverage, and I can't have that," he muttered.

Calista hated that her father couldn't be in her life, but she understood. As she glanced at her daughter, she noticed that even her daughter looked like her father. She wanted to know the next chapter in their lives as father and daughter. She felt that it just wasn't fair. She finally had a father, but because of his lifestyle, the only way he could protect her was not to be around.

"So, what's next?" Calista broke the silence.

"What's next is that I promised your mother I would get you to Atlanta, and also, you need to stop that stripping nonsense."

"How did you know I was a stripper?"

"I told you, I run these streets. Now, let's go. You and Amari have a plane to catch."

"I need a minute to talk to my mother. Can you please give me that?"

"Sure, and you can leave Amari here," he murmured.

"Why would I do that?"

"So I know you're coming back."

"Fine. I'm coming right back." Calista stormed out of the coffee shop, dialing her mother's number.

She couldn't believe after all these years, her father was alive, and her mother knew about it. It seemed like her whole life was a lie. Why would her own mother lie to her? That was the million-dollar question. The phone rang, and her mother picked up on the first ring as usual.

"Hey, baby."

"Don't 'baby' me. You knew that this nigga was alive this whole time." Calista was furious, and the tone of her voice showed it.

"Listen, Calista. You need to calm down."

"Calm down, Mom? You *lied* to me. Please, tell me, why on God's green earth would you lie to me about something as important as this?"

"Calista, you just wouldn't understand your father's lifestyle."

"Did you know he's the reason Amari's father is dead?" she whispered.

"Of course, I know."

"None of this makes sense to me."

"Calista, just get on the plane, and I'll explain it all to you when you arrive." Naomi knew she had some explaining to do.

Calista's mind was clouded with thoughts of betrayal by both her parents. She was pissed at her mom but suppressed it because she was already going through enough with her cancer treatments. She wanted to hate Freeway, but how could she when he only respected Naomi's wishes?

Calista walked back into the café and kissed her daughter on the forehead as she sat next to Freeway.

"I'm going, but I have no money for the trip at the moment," she sighed with a disappointed look. "And I have never even flown. It's on my wish list."

"Don't worry about that. I have a private jet," smirked Freeway.

"Wait—you have a private jet?" Calista smiled, slightly taken aback.

"I'm sorry, but I have to ask you something."

"Of course, you can ask me anything," he assured her.

"Are you responsible for my mother being hooked on drugs?"

"Hell no. We both lived fast lives, but she got caught up with the wrong people," frowned Freeway. "I always loved her, but she loved crack more."

"Sorry I had to ask. I can relate, even though she was a functioning addict. We always clashed when she couldn't function. There were times when I had to be the parent."

"I'm sorry you had to go through that," Freeway apologized. "Your mother and I were young and toxic together," he explained.

Freeway and his two companions walked out of Comeback Coffee on N. Main St. Freeway signaled for his driver to get the car.

"So, are you ready to see your mother and start a new life?" Freeway asked.

Calista smiled at the possibilities of a peaceful life without Amarion.

"Wait, are we going now?" She grabbed her father's arm as he walked past her.

"Yes, we're going to the General Dewitt Airport to get you to Atlanta."

"You're shitting me, right?" questioned Calista. "What about my things? I can't just leave my stuff. I have an apartment full of our belongings," she whined.

"Calista, I can get you brand-new everything when we get there. Plus, I told your mother I wasn't coming back without you," he winked.

"You going with me to Atlanta?" Calista was confused.

"We have to go," mumbled the driver.

"Well, we're ready. Let's go," Freeway told him.

"Yes, I live in Atlanta as well. Now let's get you and the baby in the car. It's getting chilly out here, plus my pilot just called."

"Okay, but I'm going to miss Memphis," she admitted.

It was all very surreal. Not only had Calista just met her father, but her father was also well off financially, and she was about to fly on a private jet. Now she was pissed that her mom had run her wealthy father out of their lives.

They all got into the car and headed to the airport to board the private jet. They drove for about thirty minutes until they arrived at General Dewitt Airport, where the plane was on a secluded airstrip.

Calista had fallen asleep during the drive. Once they arrived and began exiting the grey Suburban, Freeway woke his daughter and told her to look at the jet. She wiped her eyes as she got out of the vehicle. When she saw the jet, she had to look twice. Engraved on her father's jet were the words "*Calista's Dream*." It brought tears to her eyes to see her name emblazoned on the jet. It showed her that even though her dad was not active in her life, he never forgot her.

Chapter 19

Kendrick

Kendrick was lost in his thoughts as he sat in his classroom at Portland Community College. He had big dreams of being a major video game designer, but life had been knocking him around the last couple of months.

The police had been harassing him lately because of a case he beat after a cop pulled him over and beat him up after he left a party.

He also understood that all the weed he was smoking wasn't helping him mentally either. He always felt paranoid and was on edge, thinking somebody was always following him.

Once the professor dismissed the class, Kendrick quickly grabbed his books and headed for the exit. However, the professor stopped him before he reached the door.

The girls that walked by him waved and giggled. All of them loved Kendrick's dark skin and wavy hair, but his chiseled body really drove the ladies crazy.

"Kendrick, what's the problem? You have the highest grade in my class; however, it seems like your mind has been slipping lately." The professor removed his glasses and looked Kendrick in the eyes.

"I'm cool. I mean, after beating that case, it just seems like the whole town is looking at me differently," Kendrick said as he looked around the room. He wasn't comfortable with direct eye contact.

"You are different; you are intelligent beyond measure. What happened with you and the police was *not* your fault. Do you understand?" The professor laid his hand on Kendrick's shoulder.

Kendrick nodded and left. As he walked down the hallway, he saw Monica walking his way. He had been trying to avoid her for the last couple of days. He had been sleeping with her for about a week, and that was only for a place to stay. Ever since his mom moved to Atlanta, it left him sleeping on park benches and over at friends' houses.

Ever since her departure, he had experienced nothing but toxic relationships, one after the other. His mom was no different. She liked to drink and chase men. But she called it "having a good time." Even though she was what he referred to as "loose," his mom was still a hard worker, and because she worked hard as an IT consultant, her job transferred her to Atlanta for a higher position and better pay. So, his mom worked hard but played harder.

She had been begging her son to move in with her for weeks. Kendrick really didn't have to sleep outside or over at any female's house. It's what he chose to do. He didn't want to have his mom bail him out of trouble.

"Kendrick, have you been avoiding me?" Monica shouted as she got close to him.

"Look, Monica, not today, OK?" Kendrick sighed as he walked down the hall with his book bag on his back with one strap over his shoulder.

"Wack, bum-ass nigga," she yelled.

Kendrick just waved her off.

He exited the school building, feeling the cold air hit his face. Then finally, he noticed the bus was coming, so he ran down the sidewalk as fast as he could.

Today would not have been a good day to miss the bus, especially with the day he was having. He made it to the bus stop just in time to board the bus. He rode it for about six blocks and pulled the cord above his head when he saw his stop approaching.

Kendrick's weed stash was running low, and he desperately needed more. He got off the bus at the nearest project. No matter what hood he went to, he was very well known. Kendrick had won several awards for creating programs for video games. His future was bright in the industry.

He walked through the hood, looking to cop some green from his usual weedman. As he was searching for this connect, three guys walked up to him.

"Hey, little nigga, I think you in the wrong hood."

"Excuse me?" Kendrick turned around.

"You heard me, motherfucker," the hitta spoke with authority.

"No, I didn't hear you. What the fuck did you just say to me?" Kendrick had dedicated his life to going to college, but he was far from being a punk or soft.

"I *said,* I think you in the wrong hood."

"Well, apparently, *you* must be new out here because everybody knows who *I* am." Kendrick stood his ground.

"Well, things have changed, young boy. We're taking over now," the man said, pointing at himself and his crew.

"I don't care about that. I just want some smoke, bruh." Kendrick was getting impatient.

"Naw, it's dry down here—but we *will* take everything you got." All three of the hittas stepped forward.

Kendrick could tell these dudes were about to be a problem. He had to think quickly. Should he drop his book bag on the ground? Kendrick refused to let these guys get the upper hand on him, so he punched the guy in the face who was doing all the talking. Apparently, they were not ready. They thought Kendrick was just some square-ass guy. They didn't realize that he wasn't as soft as they thought.

After he punched the guy in the face, they all rushed him, knocked him to the ground, and started to stomp and kick Kendrick once he lay there helpless. He did his best to cover his face. But the guys didn't stop until they heard a gunshot.

When they turned around, they saw who the hood feared most. Zeke pointed his gun at them and dared them to move. These guys were not stupid. They knew who Zeke was. What they *didn't* know was that Kendrick was Zeke's nephew.

They quickly stepped away from Kendrick. They raised their hands and were shaking. They knew this was not a good look. They thought Zeke was locked up.

"OK, all three of you motherfuckers strip."

"Huh?" they said in unison.

"Did I fucking stutter, motherfuckers?" Zeke let off three rounds in the air.

The guys didn't hesitate. They started stripping. Men nearby were watching and laughing, and the soft-ass, wannabe thugs were embarrassed. Zeke pressed his gun to one of the guys' heads and gave one final warning that even they would understand loud and clear.

"If you ever come to my hood again, I will kill every last one of you. Do I make myself clear?"

They nodded and ran off. They were trying to get out of Zeke's presence as fast as possible. Kendrick was laughing . . . until he turned around and saw the grimaced look on his uncle's face. Zeke couldn't understand why the fuck his nephew had not left town to follow his mother.

"I love you, nephew, but why the fuck are you still here?" Zeke questioned.

"What do you mean? I came to get some bud." Kendrick wouldn't look his uncle straight in the eye.

"Don't play with me. You know exactly what I'm talking about." Zeke put up his gun, pulled out a blunt, lit it up, and passed it to his nephew.

"I can't keep following my mother," he told his uncle as he took a puff off the blunt.

"You got a real future ahead of you. I love you, but I can't keep looking after you," Zeke stated.

"I understand, but I never asked you to."

"You may not have asked, but you're my blood, so I'll always have your back. You are my sister's son, and I refuse to let anything happen to you if I can help it." Zeke pulled out a phone and handed it to Kendrick.

"What's this for?"

"Call your mother—now."

Kendrick knew better than to keep challenging his uncle, so he took the phone. Zeke snatched the blunt from Kendrick's hand and walked off to give him privacy. For some reason, Kendrick had a feeling his mother was expecting his call.

At first, he just stared at the phone. It shouldn't be this hard to call his mother, he thought. However, for him, it was. So he slowly began dialing her number.

"Hello," Mona answered.

"Hey, Ma." Kendrick felt nervous.

"Well, well, if it isn't the prodigal son."

"Ma, please, don't start," he groaned.

"What do you mean, 'don't start'? *You* the one running around like you don't have a mother," she fussed.

"Mom, you know I can't be around that bullshit you got going on."

"Boy, what bullshit are you referring to?"

"Please, don't make me say it." Kendrick didn't want to embarrass his mother.

"No, you know so much, so I want you to say it." Mona grew impatient.

"The men, Momma. Damn. All the men you sleep with." He felt terrible he had to say those words about his mother.

At that very moment, Mona knew why her son didn't want to be around her. He felt like she had been sleeping around with many men. Mona was incredibly beautiful. Her looks alone had guys buying her gifts. But she never removed her clothes from her body. She respected herself too much.

"First off, boy, watch your mouth. Don't ever cuss at me. I'm still your mother, and second, you must be dumb as fuck to think that of me. How *dare* you say that to me," she fumed.

After everything he had been through, he couldn't believe his mother had called him dumb.

"You must be, son, if you thought I slept with those men."

"Mom, have you forgotten? I was in the house when those guys came to your bedroom."

Kendrick shook his head as if his mom could see him.

"Kendrick, listen to what you just said . . . They came into my bedroom. Let me ask you this. How many of those men left the house mad?"

"All of them always left mad." Now that Kendrick thought about it, he had never heard any sounds of sexual activity come from his mother's room.

"Exactly. They were mad because they spent their money on me, and I never gave them anything in return but hope."

Kendrick felt like shit. For the last five years, he had thought his mom was a whore, but in reality, she was only using the guys for their money. She never slept with any of them. He sat silently on the phone for a few seconds.

"I may have been wrong for entertaining those guys, Kendrick; however, your mom was never a thot, do you hear me? I am your mother. I would never embarrass you or myself like that." Mona felt terrible because she knew she should never have brought those guys around her son in the first place. She knew that she was partially to blame for her son's thoughts.

"I apologize, Mom," Kendrick mumbled.

"Son, I love you. Now, bring your ass to Atlanta."

"What about school?"

"Kendrick, you're top of your class. You can get into any school you want. Your uncle is going to make sure you get here."

Zeke noticed that Kendrick was looking at him. He knew that was his cue. So he walked over, snatched the phone out of Kendrick's hand, and told Mona that her son would be on the next plane to Atlanta. He then ended the call.

Kendrick saw no emotion on his uncle's face. Then as his emotions toyed with his facial features, he dropped his head, attempting to hide them. "Pick your head up, boy. No matter what you think, I love you, but I can't keep looking after you."

"Uncle Zeke, I never asked you to do that."

"You're my sister's son. You're my blood, and I will always be there for you. Now, let's get you to Atlanta."

Chapter 20

Head Space

Calista couldn't believe what was going on at that moment. They were all on the private jet waiting to take off. She had never been on a plane, and having her father beside her was overwhelming. She wished her daughter was older to understand their experience at the moment. She was anxious and scared at the same time since she had never been on a plane before.

Freeway noticed his daughter's nervousness, but he saw she was excited too. He was proud he could bless her with this moment. He smiled and lit his cigar. Deep down, he wished he had been in his daughter's life. One thing was for sure . . . He wished that Naomi would've kicked her drug habit so *she* could've been in her daughter's life. Drugs had really dragged Calista's mom down an unchanging, one-way street.

Freeway never wanted to stop giving Naomi money because that money was to help take care of Calista in his absence. But since Naomi spent all the money on drugs, he had no choice but to cut her off. Freeway refused to make some low-level drug dealer rich with his money. He definitely was *not* having that.

Calista gripped the seat and began biting her lip as the jet took off.

Freeway smiled and puffed on his cigar.

When they were finally in the air, she began to relax. Freeway enjoyed being around his daughter. However, he knew it was going to end soon. His duties of being a boss on the streets would soon be active again. He wondered if his daughter knew who he was to the streets and what he did.

"Hey, baby girl."

"Yeah, what's up?" Calista said as she looked out the window.

"I need you to be completely honest with me, okay?" Freeway put out his cigar.

"Sure, why wouldn't I?" she responded, looking directly at him.

"Who do you think I am?" he asked, furrowing his brows.

"You're my father. What do you mean?" she smirked.

"No. Do you know what I do for a living?" he asked, inserting a stick of gum into his mouth.

"I don't know, but since you killed my baby daddy, are you a thug of some sort?" she retorted with a puzzled look.

"No." Freeway felt it was good his daughter didn't really know what he was.

"So, what do you do?" Now, she was curious.

"It's best if you didn't know."

"Why is that?"

"It's simple. If somebody questions you, you won't be able to answer because you don't know anything."

"Got you." Now, Calista finally understood what her father was saying.

She also understood that her father never forgot her. Calista still felt that he left because of her mom doing drugs. When she finally hit Atlanta, she planned to find out.

She knew her father had to be somebody powerful with him having a private jet, and not to mention his top hittas were terrified of him. She knew that her mom had to know something. Her father had bones in the closet, and she was going to find them.

After flying for three hours, the jet finally reached its destination. Terrified, Calista gripped the seat again as the jet touched down and began to shake. After the plane stopped, Freeway told her to grab her baby and follow him. When they stepped off the plane, a classic candy-apple-red

Lexus awaited them. Calista was very impressed with her dad's sense of style. First, he opened the door for her so she and the baby could climb in. Then he got in and signaled for the driver to pull off.

"Hey, what happened to the guy working for you when we were at the coffee shop?"

"After he dropped us off at the jet, he headed back to the city," Freeway replied as he started checking his phone emails to ensure he didn't miss any critical business opportunities.

"Why?"

"He takes care of and controls Memphis when I'm not there. Now, stop asking about my business. You've already seen too much."

Freeway didn't want his daughter to know anything about what he did. This was the only way he could keep her safe. He felt bad for his absence in her life, but, hey, what could he do? He chose this life but wanted better for the child he created, so he left and let Naomi raise her. Naomi had done a perfect job raising Calista . . . until she got on drugs.

"Before seeing your mom, I've got something for you."

"Oh really? Like what?"

"Just sit back; you'll see."

The car suddenly stopped, and the baby started crying, so Calista picked her up. Then she noticed her father had not moved. Freeway lit another cigar but quickly put it out when he remembered that his grandchild was present.

"What do you want out of life, Calista?"

"I don't know. What do you mean?"

"What are your goals? What do you want to do?"

"I don't know. I just want to be in a better position than I am currently."

"As your father, I plan on helping you to start that new position the right way."

"How do you plan on doing that?" Calista asked, smiling sarcastically.

"Get out of the car and see what I have for you." Freeway opened his door, knowing his daughter would follow.

Outside the vehicle, they stood in front of a beautiful home with a spacious yard. The house was powder blue, and colorful tulips grew alongside the sidewalk. Red drapes covered the windows. Calista thought the place was beautiful, but she had to admit she was a little confused about why she was there.

"The house is beautiful, but who lives here?"

"You do," Freeway smirked as he pulled a set of keys out of his pocket and handed them to his daughter. "Are you *serious*?" she asked. She would have been jumping up and down if she hadn't been holding Amari.

"I missed out on your whole life. And because of my lifestyle, I can't always be around, but I can make sure you have a decent place to stay." He hugged his daughter, then kissed Amari while she slept.

"I can't believe you did this for me."

"Why wouldn't I?"

"I don't know. I just didn't expect this."

"You ready to go see your mom? She's right up the street."

"Yeah, I guess so." She dropped her head down.

"Don't you want to go see her?" He was curious about her thoughts.

"Yeah, I just don't know what to expect."

They both turned around and headed back to the car. Calista was excited about the house. Now, she wondered how she would pay for the mortgage. She didn't want to lose a home that her father had put a down payment on. She had to ask him how much her monthly payments were. She also needed a job, but how could she afford day care while she worked?"How much do I need to pay a month?" She stopped walking and looked thoughtfully at her father.

"Calista, what do you mean?" He laughed.

"With the down payment you put down, how much do I have to pay monthly?"

"Calista, the house is paid for. No monthly payments are required."

They began walking again toward the car. He opened the door for his daughter once more so she could get in. Once they settled in the truck, he told the driver to pull off. So many things were running through Calista's mind. She made a lot of wrong choices in her life. What had she gotten right to deserve this blessing that the father she had just met gave her?

"Why?" she blurted out.

"Why what?"

"Why are you doing this for me?" She desperately wanted an answer.

"Why not? You're my daughter."

"I don't feel like I deserve it, that's all. Honestly, how many people get a free house?" She shrugged.

"I could say the same thing."

"How so?"

"How many fathers receive a second chance to be in their daughter's life?" Soon, the Lexus came to an abrupt stop. Then they took a sharp turn. Calista got nervous as the truck slowed and finally halted, and the engine turned off. She was the first one out of the car, trying to prepare her mind to accept seeing her mother. She had no clue what her mother's condition was at the moment, knowing her mother's drug history. Freeway saw the confused state that his daughter was in. He knew he had to coach her through this.

"It's not that big of a deal."

"What?" She was walking in circles holding Amari.

"It's not a big deal what condition she's in. This is not your fault."

"I know, but she's still my mother."

Freeway ordered his driver to stay in the car while he walked his daughter into the facility to see her recovering addict mother. When they walked into the building, the front desk lady recognized Freeway immediately. He didn't even have to sign anything. They were just pointed in the right direction. The receptionist couldn't believe how much Calista looked like her dad.

They got to Naomi's door, stopped, and looked at each other. Freeway knew something was on his daughter's mind, but he waited patiently for her to speak. But after a few moments, he finally broke the silence.

"Do you want me to go in first and see what she looks like so I can prepare you?"

"No, we can go in together." She slowly turned the knob.

When they walked in, they got the shock of their life. Naomi was sitting on the edge of her bed, looking as beautiful as ever. Calista was so happy that she handed her baby to her dad to hug her mother. Instantly, tears formed in Naomi's eyes as Calista gave her the baby to hold. "Mom, I can't believe how good you look."

"Baby, I been prayed up and staying strong," she confessed.

"When can you get out of here?"

"Now, wait a minute. Just hold up, Calista. I know she looks good, but she has to finish the program." Freeway said as he was not impressed by Naomi's appearance at all.

"Look at her, though. She looks so good."

"No, your father is right, baby. I need to follow and trust the process."

"Step outside, Calista, and let me speak with your mother." Freeway's facial expression changed suddenly.

"Fine. I need to use the bathroom anyway." She figured he had a personal matter that he had to discuss.

After the door closed, Freeway turned around to face Naomi. His smile disappeared. At first, he just stared at her. She knew what this was all about. Freeway wasted no time getting straight to the point. Naomi honestly didn't want to talk about what Freeway was about to mention. He took the baby out of her arms.

"Did you tell her?"

"No, that's not my job, Naomi."

"I appreciate you coming into her life."

"Because of your fucked-up drug habits, I had no choice." Freeway shook his head out of pity.

Naomi knew Freeway had no intentions of ever coming into his daughter's life because of his lifestyle. But he had put everything on the line to help his daughter. Naomi couldn't even look Freeway in his face. She knew it was a matter of time before her whole world would come crashing down on her. Eventually, she would have to face the music and tell her daughter what was happening.

"Naomi, when will you tell your daughter that you're dying from cancer caused by drug abuse?"

Chapter 21

Kendrick opened his eyes when he heard the pilot say they were only forty minutes out of Atlanta. He had to admit that he was nervous to see his mom; plus, he was in a whole new state. He wondered about the school he had just left. He hoped his good grades would give him entrance into a good college here. He didn't want to ignore his education because he could advance in life once he graduated. He already had pending job offers.

He thought about what he had said to his mom over the phone. She didn't admit it, but he knew she was hurt to hear her own son say and think such harsh things.

Kendrick's thoughts were cluttered as he continued to ponder. What was the first thing he wanted to say to his mother? Would he be brave enough to hug her? Who knew? Only time would tell after he landed.

Kendrick glanced at the seat across from him and saw a couple deep in love, kissing and laughing. He wanted a real love so badly. He was tired of all the one-night stands. He wondered if real love existed. It seemed like everybody had an agenda these days, which added to his trust issues.

Kendrick closed his eyes as the plane soared through the sky. He was antsy. He could feel the aircraft finally coming to a landing. His anxieties rose, not because of the landing but because he knew it was time to see his mother. Now, everybody was standing up, gathering their things. Kendrick was the last person to deplane.

He had a great flight but was unprepared for his new life in Atlanta, especially being around his mother again. He loved his mom, but she had a habit of trying to control everything around her. He refused to have his life run by her.

After getting off the plane, he waited by the conveyer belt to get his bags. He looked around to see if he could spot his mom, but there was no sign of her at the moment.

Finally, he saw his bags and grabbed them. Then he walked a few steps and took a seat. The first thing he thought was that his mom had forgotten about him. If she did, he would not be surprised one bit. He chose to give her an hour before he called her phone. He wanted to give her the benefit of the doubt. Right before he was about to give up, he heard his name called. He stood up and looked around.

"Boy, I been looking all around for you." Mona walked up and put her hands out to hug her son.

"Hey, Mom." Without realizing it, he dropped his bags and hugged his mother.

He forgot how warm his mother's hugs were. Mona kept saying over and over how much she missed him. By her greeting, he felt she had been missing him and truly loved him. They both looked at each other, understanding that they'd been missing out on building a bond for the last two years that they'd been apart. After they finished hugging, they walked outside to depart from the airport. Mona got to the parking lot and hit the unlock button on her key fob. Kendrick couldn't believe his mother was driving a 2020 Mercedes-Benz. He was in awe.

"What the hell, Mom?" His jaw dropped at the surprise.

"Nice, isn't it, son?"

"Damn right, this is nice. But wait, Mom, is this some guy's car you driving?" Of course, he had to ask, knowing her history of using men.

"Listen to me, son. When I tell you this is my shit, it's my shit. Now, get in the car. I got a surprise for you." She popped the trunk to put her son's suitcases inside.

They both got into the car, and Mona pulled off. Kendrick was looking at the lovely scenery as they were driving. He had no idea what the surprise was that his mother had in store for him. He was begging God that she wouldn't have him meet some guy and say she was getting married. He tried his best to clear his mind and keep his thoughts in a positive light.

They pulled into a parking lot to what he could gather was a place that sold pastries. He couldn't believe this was the surprise his mother had for him.

"Really, Mom, pastries?" He shook his head.

"Just get out of the car, Kendrick."

He unbuckled his seat belt with an attitude as he sucked his teeth and opened the door. He wasn't in the mood for no damn pastries. His mom walked around the car. She started giggling because she could tell he had an attitude. Then she put her arm around his shoulders, giving him a half hug.

"Boy, what's wrong with you?"

"Mom, you brought me here to buy me a pastry like I'm some kid?" he said, refusing to look at her.

"See, that's your problem. You see what you want to see. But you're not looking at the full picture of things," she explained.

"Mom, there is no full picture here. Face it. You brought me to a pastry shop like I should be excited."

Mona grabbed her son's chin and made him look at the title of the building. It read "*Kendrick's Pastries.*" He realized his name was in the title. He walked away from his mom to look closer at the building. He was speechless at that moment.

"Do you know the owner or something? How'd you get my name on the building?"

"Come on, let's take a walk inside." Mona grabbed her son's hand.

Kendrick noticed how nice the building was. It was shaped like a pastry. It was pretty clever, he thought. When they got to the door, the door handles were shaped like spoons, which he also thought was innovative and creative.

When they stepped inside, all the workers looked at Mona and said, "Hey, boss."

It blew Kendrick away.

"Mom, this is *your* shop?"

"Yeah, one of them." She smiled.

"*One* of them? You mean you have *more* shops?"

"The surprise is, when you're ready, this shop is yours."

"Mom, I'm confused. How did all this happen?"

"Well, I was late on my bills, and I started baking for extra money. Before I knew it, people wanted my pastries like crazy. My apartment started to become too small for all the orders that I was getting. So, I took out a loan. Long story short, I bought a building, made colossal money, paid my loan back, and here we are."

"So, this shop right here is mine?" he asked. He couldn't believe how long the line was just for three pastries.

"Son, look at me. You still will graduate school."

"Of course, Ma."

Mona took a step back and let her son enjoy the moment.

Being from the hood, he had never seen anything like this. He could not believe his mother had all this and never told him. Then he wondered why she hadn't told him. After all his struggles and problems, she didn't inform him she was now a successful business owner.

"Hey, Mom, this is nice and all, but I can't help but wonder why you didn't tell me you had all of this." He turned to look at her.

"The answer is simple, son. Because I wanted you to come here on your own."

He looked at her face and saw nothing but honesty. She didn't want to influence his decision with her business. She wanted him to come back to her on his own.

Kendrick didn't realize that some of the women working behind the counter were eyeballing him in a very sexy way. Mona recognized it and addressed it right away.

"Listen, ladies, this is your boss, and my son is off-limits to everyone." She giggled after her statement.

"Ma, why you got to announce that?"

"Because these women are looking at you like you a damn snack. Son, you are not to sleep with your employees."

"Mom, you *do* realize that I'm grown, right?" Kendrick stuck out his chest in a macho way.

"Son, you *do* realize this is a business, right?" She stared at him.

"Mom, I got this."

"Whatever. Come back to the office and let's talk business before I show you the second surprise."

"Wait . . . There's more?"

"Yup." She began to walk toward the back.

As they went, Kendrick watched all the bakers preparing the many pastries. Some were chocolate, strawberry, and even a mixture of flavors he had never seen before. His mother designed pastries with character faces like SpongeBob and even the classic Bugs Bunny. She had done things to pastries that he had never seen done before. It was no wonder that her business was a success. Finally, they entered a huge, comfortable office.

"Take a seat, son."

"OK." He could tell this was serious.

"Now, son, I'll be frank with you. This is your shop."

"But? I know there's a catch to this."

"You're right. There is a catch to this. I want you to finish school first."

"I knew this was too good to be true."

"Hear me out. I want you to work in the shop so you can get familiar with how things operate. Meanwhile, I'll be working on getting you back in school."

"But I'm the boss, right?""Of course you are. Now, let's go to see the other surprise."

They got up with an understanding of the conversation that they had just had. Kendrick wanted to finish school, but he also wanted to be a boss too. So he followed his mom outside and got into the luxury car he had arrived in. Now he was wondering what in the world the next surprise could be. Even though they were both excited to be around each other, they rode silently. Both of them had a lot on their minds.

They pulled up to an amazing, breathtaking, three-story brick house. Once again, Kendrick could not believe his eyes. Immediately, he knew that it had to be his mom's house. She told him to follow her around back. When they reached the rear of the house, they saw a vast swimming pool filled with clear, beautiful water.

"Mom, this is amazing. I like it."

"I appreciate it, son. I really do."

Mona took a seat on the small step that led to the pool. She gazed at her son, and tears began to fall. Kendrick had no idea why his mom was crying. She had everything she wanted, so why the hell was she crying?

He put his hand on her shoulder to calm her nerves. She gently patted his hand while wiping her tears away with her other free hand.

"Mom, what's wrong? You have it all right now."

"That may be true, but you struggled while I lived well over here. But I wanted you to come here on your own terms so that you wouldn't have to struggle like I have."

"Mom, come on. I understand completely." Kendrick gave her an assuring smile as he helped wipe away her tears.

"I was the one that sent the money to your uncle for a lawyer to fight your case against that crooked cop."

"Yeah, that was a rough time in my life," Kendrick replied as anger filled his heart just thinking about the situation that had taken place with the police.

"It's OK, though, because it's all behind us now. So let's focus on new beginnings. Also, the money that your pastry shop makes will help to go toward your schooling."

"Damn, really?"

"Son, I told you . . . I got you." Mona reached her hand out so her son could help her up.

They both went into the house to unwind.

Chapter 22

Invisible

Kendrick was sitting at the table enjoying a home-cooked meal that consisted of baked potatoes and steak smothered in gravy that his mom had cooked. She kept telling him to slow down, but it had been a long time since he had eaten a meal like that. While he was eating, a million things ran through his mind. He couldn't believe that he was actually thinking about giving up school. What did he need school for now? Ever since his mother showed him that pastry shop and told him it was his, all he wanted to do was be a boss.

He finished his dinner, washed his plate, and walked into the living room. It had all-white carpeting and plush, white and tan furniture.

Mona was on a business call to get a new location for her fifth pastry shop. Kendrick was trying to get her attention, but she put up her index finger as if to say, "Hold on." So, he just sat beside her.

She quickly tapped him on the shoulder and told him to find a pen.

He walked into the kitchen and looked through all the drawers for a pen when he came across a sticky note that read: "*You got one week to pay back the loan.*" This was not a business letter from the bank. It had him wondering who she really obtained the loan from. Finally, he found a pen, walked back over to her, and handed it to her as he sat beside her.

Should he mention the note that he found? Why would she lie? He had to know the truth. He waited until she was off the phone. She finally hung up.

"Finding good locations is starting to become hard, son." She wiped her forehead as if she had sweat dropping down.

"How fast did you pay off the loan, Ma?" He waited to see if he would get an honest answer.

"About two weeks. Then I paid off the bank."

"Would you lie to me?" He started tapping his foot on the white carpet.

"Boy, why would I lie to you?" She looked very nervous.

Angrily, Kendrick stormed back into the kitchen and pulled out the drawer that contained the sticky note. He grabbed it and hurried back to where his lying mother was sitting. He slung the note on the table.

Mona looked at the note in disbelief. She had forgotten to toss it. She picked up the note, balled it up, and threw it across the floor. Kendrick couldn't believe her actions at that moment.

"Have you lost your mind going through my shit?"

"Have you lost your mind lying to me?" He stood his ground.

"This is grown folks' business. You wouldn't understand."

"*Excuse you?* I *am* grown. Or have *you* forgotten?"

"Son, I advise you to sit down and get out of my face."

"With all this money you're making, why haven't you repaid this person?"

"Because it's my personal business and has nothing to do with you. Don't worry. Your shop is yours, and you have nothing to be concerned about."

"Are you crazy? Our safety could be in jeopardy if you borrowed from the wrong person." Kendrick started pacing around.

He could not believe the nerve of his mother. Did he travel here to be put in some more mess? He couldn't even look at her right then. He walked back into the kitchen and took a seat. Mona knew her son was feeling some type of way since he had run the streets at one point. Going to college is what took him out of the streets. Kendrick also lost his father to the streets. She soon followed her son into the kitchen.

"Kendrick, we don't need this friction between us."

"I don't know what to say," he muttered.

"I have everything under control; trust me."

"That's just it. It's not that I *don't* trust you. The person you borrowed the money from is who I don't trust."

"This guy has plenty of money."

"Ma, what does that mean?" Kendrick shook his head.

"It means he has plenty of money and will not miss it at all." She sat down at the kitchen table.

"What the fuck?" Kendrick jumped out of his seat.

"Boy, you better watch your mouth."

"You worried about my mouth, but what you *need* to be worried about is *yourself*. If you borrowed money from a street nigga, Mom, there's *going* to be a problem."

"I'm your mother, and you need to watch your mouth."

"I don't want to be in your mess, Mom!"

"You won't be. Just trust me on this." She attempted to reassure him.

Kendrick rolled his eyes and walked out of the kitchen. He could not be in the house another minute. He walked through the living room and out the front door. He desperately needed some fresh air. This whole situation concerned him. Then he heard his mom call his name.

"Kendrick, Kendrick." Mona came storming out of the house.

"What, Ma? Please, give me some space."

"Listen, we don't need to be fighting. You just got here, OK?" She kissed her son on the cheek.

"OK, but I better not get caught up in your mess."

"I promise you that my actions will not come back on you. I promise you're overthinking the situation."

"If you say so, Ma."

"How about you take the car and get familiar with your pastry shop?"

"You serious?"

"Of course." She smiled and handed him the keys.

Kendrick kissed his mother and ran toward the driveway to jump into the luxury car. He wasted no time sticking the key in the ignition. He backed the car up while waving at his mother. Just because she let him use the car, he was not letting go of the fact that she owed somebody money. If he had to guess, it was no small-time guy.

Kendrick drove down the street with his windows down. He wanted people to see him. He felt big time. Maybe being in Atlanta wasn't going to be so bad after all . . . other than the fact that there was some rogue that his mom owed money to. What he couldn't get out of his mind was that he knew his mom had the money to pay whomever this person was.

Kendrick got to the pastry shop and parked. He rolled up the windows, stepped out of the car, and stared at the building. He still couldn't believe the pastry shop belonged to him.

Kendrick shook it off. He had to get that bullshit off his mind. Walking in, he noticed that some guy was staring at him. Kendrick stopped in his tracks and stared back. The guy looked at Kendrick and started laughing. Kendrick was not about to put up with disrespect, so he made his way over to the mystery man.

The man had his arms folded, leaning up against his Mustang. When Kendrick got close, the guy took out a cigarette and lit it. He smiled after taking a puff of the Newport and blew the smoke in Kendrick's face. Kendrick smacked the cigarette out of his hand, surprising the man with his actions.

"Dude, have you lost your goddamn mind?" the guy snapped at Kendrick.

"Naw, but I think you have by the way you fucking with me."

"Look, man, I'm just waiting for the owner to show up." He laughed.

"What the fuck you want with the owner?"

"I'm not trying to be rude, but that's none of your damn business, so why don't you be a good little nigga and go find the owner."

"Hey, new boss," the cashier who saw Kendrick earlier yelled.

"Hey. I'll be there in a minute," Kendrick said politely.

The guy's eyes widened when he heard the girl announce Kendrick as the new boss. To him, Kendrick did not look like he would own a pastry shop. The stranger grew a little nervous, so he pulled out another Newport. Kendrick smacked that cigarette out of his hand too.

"Yo, now, what's your deal?" the guy spat out.

"You said you was looking for the owner. Well, here I am. Now, what the hell you want?"

"I don't know if you realize it, but all businesses have to pay for protection on this street."

Kendrick smirked at the man, who he assumed was Italian.

"Yo, Pauli, Vinnie, whatever your fucking name is. It's *not* happening," frowned Kendrick.

Frustrated, the man rubbed his hand over his slicked-back hair and down his chubby face.

"You serious?"

"Afraid so. New monkey on the block."

Kendrick took a step back, looked at the man, laughed at him, and strolled away. But the guy's face contorted as he bit his lip and rubbed his hands together. Kendrick's nonchalant attitude had pissed him off. Not only did Kendrick ignore his "request," but he also laughed at him.

The guy yelled at Kendrick, calling him all types of niggas. Kendrick still ignored him and kept walking. The guy then called Kendrick's mother a "nigga whore" . . . which got his attention.

"I guess your nigga-whore-ass momma gon' be paying the protection money for you."

"What the fuck did you just say?" Kendrick asked as he turned around.

"You heard me. I'll get my money one way or another."

Now, it got personal when the guy insulted Kendrick's mom by calling her out her name and threatening her. Kendrick hit him with a flurry of punches. Next, he grabbed him and threw him over the hood of his own Cadillac. Kendrick quickly walked to the other side of the car and kicked the guy in the stomach. After that, he reached down and grabbed him by his throat. Again, he hit him with a flurry of haymakers.

"Nigga, if you *ever* come here again, I will end you," Kendrick warned, punching him two more times. The guy hit the pavement face-first—hard. His face was swollen and leaking blood. "What you say your name was again?" spat Kendrick as he rolled the guy onto his back.

"Your black ass just fucked up," he growled as blood ran from his broken nose and mouth.

He crawled to the other side of his car and stood. After getting into it, he sped out of the parking lot. Kendrick shook his head and dusted himself off. Finally, he headed inside his very own pastry shop. When he walked in, all eyes were on him. Everybody saw what he had just done on the camera that had a view of the parking lot.

As the new guy, he knew he owed the crew an apology, but an old guy stopped him when he was about to apologize for what had just transpired.

"Don't you do it, youngblood." He chewed tobacco while rubbing his long, grey beard.

"Don't do what?"

"Don't apologize for getting rid of that no-good-ass wetback. He been harassing people for the last year or so now. That ass whooping was overdue," the man laughed.

"Who are you, sir?"

"Oh, my name's Mr. Benson. I handle the maintenance work and fix the ovens and whatever else needs to be fixed. It's a pleasure to meet you, boss." He shook Kendrick's hand.

"Great, nice to meet you, Mr. Benson."

"The pleasure is all mines, youngblood."

"Please follow me to the office, Mr. Benson."

They walked through the kitchen area so they could go to the office. Once they both walked inside, Kendrick closed the door behind them. He had a few quick questions to which he felt Mr. Benson might know the answers.

"I need to ask you something if you don't mind."

"Sure, shoot your question at me." He still was chewing his tobacco, spitting in his spit cup.

"Do you know who my mom got the loan from to start the pastry business?"

"Youngblood, I can't spill the beans on your mother like that, but I can tell you he is a very ruthless man. If she hasn't paid him, she needs to."

"Is that right?"

"Oh yeah. This dude's been running shit for over twenty years. If he wants his money, he will come to collect."

"Thank you, Mr. Benson."

"No problem, youngblood."

Kendrick was concerned about who this person was, and it sounded like he operated by a strict street code. His mom needed to come clean and pay him his money.

Chapter 23

Energy

When Calista walked back into the room, she noticed some tension was building. She could feel that the vibe was off between her parents. So she took her baby from her father.

"Is everything all right?" Calista asked with concern.

"Everything is cool. Let me talk to you right quick before I go, and, Naomi, do the right thing," Freeway scolded.

"OK, sure thing," Calista responded to her father but was looking at her mother.

They both walked outside the room into the hallway. Freeway paced back and forth. He was angry and confused as old feelings resurfaced, but he couldn't let it show. Instead, he looked at his daughter with concern.

"Look, baby girl, you can keep the car. The driver and I will take an Uber. If you need me or have an emergency, call me." He pulled out a piece of paper and a pen, wrote down his number, and gave it to Calista.

"What's wrong?" she asked. She could tell her dad's energy was different.

"Just talk to your mom. I got to go. Remember, call me if you need me."

Freeway hugged and kissed Calista and his granddaughter.

"I will. I really need answers," she frowned.

"I understand. So do I. But some things are best not known," he whispered, walking off.

Calista felt perplexed about seeing her father walk away, but she smiled as she realized there was a bright side. She had a car and a house, thanks to him. She watched him disappear down the hallway. When he was gone, she returned to her mom's room. She planned to pick her mom's brain for answers about Freeway.

When she entered the room, she laid Amari on the bed, then sat on the edge of the bed, grabbed her mother's hands, and looked into her eyes. Her mother looked sober, and her skin was glowing. But she noticed how her mother never made eye contact. Naomi quickly looked away, like she was ashamed of her past indiscretions.

"Okay, Mom, what's the deal here?" She released Naomi's hand and looked at her.

"Calista, I don't know what you're talking about," she lied. She again looked away. Her expression was blank.

"Oh, you know something. Freeway has a private jet with my name on it, and on top of that, he gave me a house and a Benz. For a man that just walked back into my life, that's a lot. Now, tell me who he is."

"I see he went all out." Naomi furrowed her eyebrows. Her anxieties rose as she again felt like she had been selfish to have barred Cal from being a father. Maybe his presence would have made up for her lack of presence.

Naomi had no clue that Freeway had done all this for Calista. She was speechless at Freeway embracing his role as a father. She knew Calista wanted answers. She promised Freeway that if he helped her, she would not reveal his past. She couldn't bring up old wounds and mental scars. It was tough enough to look at her daughter, especially since she knew that she would soon be dying.

"What is that supposed to mean?"

"Just surprised that he spent that much money."

"Why? I *am* his daughter, *right?*"

"Why must you question a blessing? Ask *him*," sighed Naomi.

"I'm trying to understand who he is, so tell me."

"I can't; ask him." Naomi kept her head down.

"Whatever answers you need, he can tell you," she mumbled. "Be honest with yourself, Calista. How many Black men you know own private jets?"

Calista had to think long and hard about that and the things he had bought her in a short time. That was a lot of cash being thrown out. But on the other hand, why was her mother so shocked that he spent that type of money on her? A lot was going on, and she felt left in the dark about it. Her daddy wouldn't tell her shit, and her mother wasn't telling her shit. She needed to clear her mind so badly.

"I have one question."

"Calista, I will try to answer it the best I can." She felt bad she couldn't give her daughter the answers her heart desired.

"Why are you so surprised that he spent that money on me?" Calista was hoping she could at least get that answered.

"Because your father don't play when it comes to his money."

"Damn, really?" Calista could tell that her father was a no-nonsense man who was not wasteful by her mother's statement.

"Yes, honey, he is very determined and focused, and that's why he stayed out of your life. It wasn't that he didn't love you because he did. But being who he was, he just couldn't be in your life."

Calista's mind started racing. Maybe it was a good thing that he wasn't in her life. She was a firm believer that everything happened in God's timing. After Amarion, she was just glad to experience some normalcy. Whatever Freeway lacked as a father, he was definitely making up as a grandfather.

"I need a place to clear my head." She felt overwhelmed and disappointed.

"A brand-new pastry shop just opened up down the street," Naomi suggested.

"Amari is asleep. Can you watch her for a couple of hours?"

"Sure. Go have some downtime."

"OK. Just give me a few hours, and I'll be back, I promise."

"No worries. Take your time."

Calista left her mom and headed out of the building. She walked through the parking lot, looking for the car that her father had left for her. Finally, she spotted it in the third row. She opened the unlocked driver's-side door and sat in the driver's seat, instantly searching for the keys. She looked under the seat, then in the glove compartment. No luck. She looked up and flipped down the visor. The keys fell into her lap.

Excited, she stuck them in the ignition and drove out of the hospice center parking lot, looking for the pastry shop her mom had spoken of. She drove a few miles and found it not far from the facility. She eased into the parking lot and parked. After getting out of the car, she checked out the building and its bright sign.

"Nice," she said to herself.

She slowly walked toward the door, appreciating the color scheme of the place. It was very eye-catching. Soon, she sat at a table and was blown away when she realized there was a menu for pastries. She opened the menu and saw over forty different types. She never knew that so much could be done with a pastry.

Kendrick walked out of the office to grab a menu to start familiarizing himself with his product. Calista was sitting at the table when chills suddenly went through her body. She looked up and immediately locked eyes with Kendrick. He smiled and walked by. The feeling she was experiencing was new to her. However, when she looked back at Kendrick, she no longer saw him. He had already walked around and made it to the other side.

Ain't no way that man made me feel like this simply by walking past me, she thought. Now, her mind was all over the place. She looked around to see if she saw the mystery man who had just walked by her, but he was nowhere to be found. This was impossible. She felt like she was in a movie. Quickly, she glanced back at the menu but couldn't focus.

She found the pastry she wanted to order, so she sashayed to the front counter.

"Get it together," she told herself. She stood second in line and was next to order. She couldn't believe how many people were in there just for pastries.

"Hi. Welcome to Kendrick's Pastries. What are you having today?" the cashier said with a blinding-white smile.

"I would like to order the blueberry tart, please," Calista replied.

"Just one?" asked the cashier.

"Yes, please, and thank you." Calista was very polite as she took in the color scheme and cleanliness of the shop.

"It will be right up."

"Thank you," smiled Calista.

Calista stood and waited on her order. She felt like she was acting foolish. She was so deep in her thoughts that she didn't hear the girl trying to hand her what she had just ordered. Then the girl tapped her on the shoulder.

"Here's your order," she said, handing her the bag.

"Oh shit, thank you. I apologize."

Calista took her pastry back to the table. She thought about the number her dad had given her. She wanted to know if he got that Uber. She took the number out of her pocket, stared at the paper,

then put it away. Her father said, "for emergencies only." So she figured she'd better respect his
wishes.

She opened her bag and pulled out the pastry. It
was large. She picked at the icing, smiling, as it was
sweet and delicious. As she bit into the pastry, she
moaned. It was so moist that she felt like her taste
buds were dancing. After she finished eating it, she
decided to go outside. She truly enjoyed the nice
cool breeze blowing on her face.

"Damn, shorty, you sexy." A guy walked up behind her and smacked her on the ass.

"Nigga, don't fucking touch me."

"Come on, don't be like that, big booty." He
smiled, flashing his gold fronts.

"*Excuse me?* Is *this* how you talk to women?" she
said, angry.

"Why you acting like that, sweetheart?" He
grabbed her hand and ran it over his dick.

"Get the fuck off me!" She snatched her hand
back.

"Bitch, you know who I am?" He grabbed her by
the throat as he inched closer.

Calista tried to push him off her. Then he kissed
her on the cheek. Calista looked around, but nobody was outside. She tried to scream, but his grip
on her throat was so tight, nothing came out. Now,
he slapped her, and she dropped to her knees.

Mr. Benson happened to walk outside to clean
the parking lot and saw Calista in trouble.

"Hey, motherfucker, get your hands off that girl!" he yelled.

Even though he knew he was no match for the attacker, he had to try. He had lost his daughter to a rapist.

"Get the fuck back inside, old man, before I fuck you up," the guy threatened.

Mr. Benson knew precisely what he had to do. He ran inside as fast as his old legs would carry him, got to the office, and begged Kendrick to come outside. Kendrick tried to calm him, but Mr. Benson kept grabbing his arm, pulling him toward the door.

"Come on, move your ass, youngin'." He was still pulling on Kendrick.

"Calm down! What's going on?"

"Kendrick, we have to go. A girl's in trouble."

When Kendrick heard that, he finally rose out of his seat and quickly followed Benson outside, where they saw the guy had pushed Calista against the wall, choking her. Kendrick ran over and grabbed him from behind.

"So, you like beating on women, huh?" he barked.

"You don't want these problems, bruh," the man smirked as he held Calista in his grasp. Now, he pushed her to the ground.

"Now, wassup, bitch-ass nigga?" yelled Kendrick as he grabbed the guy.

Kendrick smashed him into the wall headfirst. After that, he grabbed him and threw him against the wall, repeatedly punching him in the face. Finally, he made the guy apologize to Calista, then dragged him out to the parking lot and threw him in the street, off his property. Kendrick quickly walked over and helped Calista off the ground. When she grabbed his hand, an unknown energy shot through their bodies. They both felt it. It sent goose bumps running all over their skin. The energy was so powerful that Calista jerked her hand back out of fear. She jumped to her feet and ran to her car. Kendrick just watched as she drove away. Shit, Kendrick couldn't blame her because the energy was also puzzling to him. "What was that about?" Mr. Benson asked.

Chapter 24

Changes

Calista drove fast as she could back to the hospice center where her mom and daughter were. The altercation at the pastry shop freaked her the hell out. She had never before experienced anything like that in her life. She knew it was rude to run away after being saved, but what was she to do after experiencing *that?*

Calista needed to get to a place where she could regain her composure. She wanted so desperately to hold her daughter at that moment. Instead, she was a nervous wreck. The attack brought back memories of Amarion and how he made her feel helpless. She turned a hard left to enter the facility's parking lot, quickly parked the car, and didn't hesitate to enter the facility, where she felt a sense of safety.

She ran down the hall and barged into her mom's room when she got into the building. Then she jumped on the bed, grabbed her baby girl, and hugged her tightly. Naomi was sitting in her rocking chair reading the Bible. She knew right away that something wasn't right with her daughter. She tried her best to wait for Calista to say something. Instead, Calista just lay with her daughter in silence.

"Baby, are you all right?" asked a concerned Naomi.

"I hate Atlanta. I need to go back to Memphis." Calista spoke incoherently.

"Calista, you haven't given this place a chance," responded Naomi.

"I did give this place a chance—until I almost got raped," she answered as her eyes widened and tears streamed down her face.

"What? You got attacked?" asked a shocked Naomi as she set her Bible on the table next to her. "Dear God, thank you for protecting my daughter."

"That's what I said. Luckily, someone fought the guy off," she murmured. Her mind drifted off to how Amarion used to force her to have sex with him.

Finally, Calista sat up on the edge of the bed, contemplating whether she had made a hasty decision to move to Atlanta. She knew she needed to return and properly show the guy who saved her that she was thankful. It was rude the way she left. She sat her baby on the bed to let her play, got off the bed, and kissed her mom on the forehead, knowing what happened wasn't her fault.

"You OK, baby girl?" asked Naomi as tears flowed from her eyes.

"Not really, but I got to go back and thank the men that saved me," said a slightly less-shaken Calista.

"OK, but please, be safe," emphasized Naomi.

"I will, and I'll be right back."

"Calista, take your time."

Once again, Calista left her mom's room to exit the building. When she was in her car, she just sat there for a few minutes, still slightly shaken.

Before starting the car, she had to figure out what she would do to express her gratitude. She was trying to calm her nerves before returning. Finally, she stuck the key in the ignition and pulled off.

The closer she got to the pastry shop, the more anxious she became. Her heart felt like it was beating out of her chest. Finally, she reached her destination and eased into the parking lot. Before she exited the car, she sat in silence for a moment. Paranoia set in as she cautiously looked about her. Then slowly, she opened her door and stepped out. Hastily, she went into the building. Once she was inside, she sat. She had to get herself together before she even tried speaking to anybody.

"Hey, are you all right?" asked a cashier who approached Calista with genuine concern.

"Yeah, you saw what happened?" Calista felt embarrassed.

"Yeah, girl. I saw the aftermath. That was some bullshit."

"I wouldn't wish that on anyone," murmured Calista, looking away.

"Oh no, girl, you are *not* to blame," said the cashier. "By the way, my name's Cleo. If you need anything, let me know."

"I want to thank the guy that saved me."

"That was Kendrick, the owner," smiled Cleo.

"Can you let him know I'd like a word with him, please?"

"Sure, no problem. I'll get him. Sit tight," Cleo said as she walked off.

Even though it was not her fault, Calista felt like it was. She felt like she had embarrassed herself and had been distracted. The bigger problem was what she would say to this guy once he was back in front of her. Suddenly, she looked up and noticed the man walking in her direction.

"Hi." Kendrick stuck out his hand.

"If you don't mind, I'd rather not shake hands," Calista said reluctantly.

"Hey, it's cool." Kendrick put his hand down.

"I just came back to thank you and apologize for rushing off," she said.

"May I join you?" asked Kendrick.

"Sure, why not." Calista slid over so he could get into the booth.

When he sat down, she got extremely nervous and didn't know why. She picked up the menu to calm her nerves. Kendrick wasn't nervous at all. Calista started humming to herself, something that she did to calm herself.

"So, why did you run away?" he inquired.

"Because I guess I was afraid," she replied.

"Scared of what?" His face softened.

"I guess the trauma of almost getting raped rattled me." She frowned.

"And I caused a disturbance here."

"It wasn't your fault that he was a busta-ass nigga," Kendrick assured her.

"I still feel guilty," she said as she dropped her head.

Calista realized that her nerves were everywhere, so she excused herself. She scooted past him and, again, felt their attraction. Her heart rate increased, and her palms were clammy. She hurried into the bathroom and splashed cold water on her face, telling herself to get it together.

Kendrick sat back down as he took in how beautiful Calista was. He couldn't describe the feelings that were running through his body. He began to tap his fingers on the table until he saw Calista come out of the bathroom. He could tell she felt a little uncomfortable for some reason. He immediately got up so she could sit back down.

"I don't even know your name," Kendrick joked, his way to clear the awkwardness between them.

"I'm Calista. It's nice to meet you," she smiled.

"I'm Kendrick. Nice to meet you as well, Calista."

"Your name is Kendrick?" She thought about the name of the building she was sitting in. "I thought the older guy was the owner," she said.

"No, that's Mr. Benson. He's the one who alerted me of the situation," smiled Kendrick.

"Well, I am grateful to you both," she said.

"So, I guess you're a Black man who still believes in protecting Black women?" she asked as she fiddled with her hair.

"I see no reason for a man to ever put his hands on a Black woman or any woman," smiled Kendrick.

"Yeah, me either."

They both began to get comfortable and started talking. Kendrick even grabbed her hand several times. They both felt the energy, but it just felt right. They were slowly learning about each other, even talking about their hometowns. Calista told Kendrick about her daughter, Amari. Before you knew it, two hours had gone by. Now, Kendrick held her hand and walked outside.

"You telling me somebody as beautiful as you doesn't have a man?" he asked, looking directly into her eyes.

"No, I attract assholes," she said, gazing up into his eyes.

"It's crazy, but I'm feeling you," said Kendrick looking at her.

"I don't want to be hurt. My daughter's father said the same shit. He used to beat my ass just to have something to do." She looked down at the ground.

"I would never put my hands on you," he assured her.

He took his finger and put it under her chin to lift her head gently so she could see that he was being sincere.

She looked at him, and they both felt the instant mental attraction that they had. They were holding hands and couldn't let go. Kendrick had to know; he had to ask.

"Please, tell me you're feeling what I'm feeling," he whispered.

"I felt it the first time you touched my hand," she smiled.

"It didn't scare you?" He needed to know.

"Hell yeah, it scared me. How about you?"

"It definitely felt weird."

"I love where this conversation is going. How about you?" she asked.

"Why wouldn't I?" He wrapped his arms around her.

It felt as if they had known each other for years. Neither of them wanted the moment to end. They were in a moment where time felt like it stood still. It didn't feel like it would end . . . until Kendrick's phone rang.

"Hello," he answered.

"Hey, where are you? Come pick me up," Mona requested.

"Just talking to a new friend." He looked at Calista and smiled.

"Bring your friend with you. I need to go to the bank," she said.

"OK, I'm on my way," he responded.

"Hey, are you okay with following me to my mother's house?" Kendrick asked.

"You sure? Let me call my mother so she won't be worried." Calista felt skeptical about going, but she checked on Amari and her mother. "I'm new here, so let's exchange numbers first, just in case I get lost," she said.They exchanged numbers. Then Kendrick went to his car, and Calista went to hers to follow him. They both pulled out of the parking lot. She was awestruck that she had just met Kendrick and was already about to meet his mom. She kept thinking that it wasn't the norm. But she was adapting to new things.

Kendrick pulled into the driveway while Calista cautiously parked on the side curb. Then just in case things didn't go right, she could pull off quickly.

Maybe she was thinking too negatively, she thought.

Mona was sitting on the step, waiting on Kendrick to arrive. He got out of his car.

"Hey, Ma, you ready?" he questioned.

"Kendrick, I don't recognize that car from the job. I thought I knew all my employees' vehicles," she frowned. Mona was staring at the car and waiting to see who got out.

"She doesn't work at the shop. She got attacked leaving our place," he explained.

"Son, we don't need that type of attention at our business." Mona got a hard look at Calista when she stepped out of the car.

"Hello. Nice to meet you," Calista said, smiling when she walked up.

"Oh, fuck no. Kendrick get her ass off my property," Mona yelled.

"Mom, what's your damn problem?" Kendrick boomed.

"She looks like a damn slut. Get her ass away from me," yelped Mona.

"Excuse me, but it takes one to know one." Calista was offended by Mona's harsh words. She stood back with her arms folded, frowning at Mona.

"Bitch, you heard me. Get the fuck off my property before I call the police," reiterated Mona as she waved her iPhone.

"Kendrick, I don't need this bullshit." Calista stormed down the sidewalk, got into her car, and drove off.

Kendrick was furious. He couldn't believe his mom acted that way toward somebody she had never met. He ran after Calista down the driveway, but she faded down the street. Angry, he walked back up the driveway, giving his mother a stern look.

"What?" Mona rolled her eyes.

"What do you mean, 'what'? Why would you treat her like that?"

"Son, you don't want to get involved with a woman like that."

"Mom, you know nothing about her."

"Let me ask you one question, Kendrick."

"What?"

"Does she have a baby?" She gave her son a stern look.

"Yeah, she does, but so what?"

"You have a bright future in business and school. You don't need a woman like that to bring you down."

"You know what, Mom?"

"What?" She put her hands on her hips.

"You watch too much damn Lifetime. Right now, I can't deal with you. You call me when you're ready to apologize to Calista and me." Kendrick took off, walking down the street.

Mona yelled at him, but he was so angry that he completely ignored her. She couldn't believe how her son went against her for a girl he had just met. Then again, she had no idea of the energy Calista and Kendrick shared. Not even a mother's love would be able to come between a connection so deep that it burned like fierce flames. Mona shook her head and walked back into the house. She had to figure out how to get her son back.

As Kendrick was walking down the street, he pulled out his phone to call Calista. But she pulled behind him and blew the horn before he could dial her number. His heart began to melt when he turned around and saw Calista's face.

Chapter 25

In the Clouds

Kendrick opened the door and got in. He was about to apologize for his mom's behavior, but Calista grabbed him and kissed him seductively. It felt like the Fourth of July in her car as their bodies ignited with the flame of love. Kendrick's heart felt like it was about to burst out of his chest.

"Did you feel that?" Calista asked.

"Hell yeah, I felt that," Kendrick said, trying to cool himself down.

"Me too. I felt it the first time you grabbed my hand. At first, it scared me, but now, it feels like great energy."

"Now what?" Kendrick strapped on his seat belt.

"Right now, you get to meet *my* daughter and mom because I need to pick up my baby. My mom is at a hospice facility. Is that OK?"

"Yeah, I hope your mom acts better than my mom did." Kendrick shook his head, still embarrassed by his mother's rude behavior.

They drove off to pick up Amari. Kendrick couldn't fight the feelings he felt for Calista. Damn, was this even real? He thought how his mom played with love had given him trust issues for years. Were women trustworthy, and could he fall in love in one day? But as far as he knew, these feelings were real.

"Hey, let me ask you something." He touched her lightly while she held the steering wheel.

"What's up?" She was anxious to know what was on his mind.

"I don't want you to think I'm crazy, but I think I love you," Kendrick said nervously, unaware of Calista's response. He didn't want to seem crazy. After all, they had just met.

"Well, I guess we're both kind of crazy because I think I love you too." She smiled to let Kendrick know it was OK to feel that way.

"Really, Calista? Are you serious?"

"Yes, I wouldn't lie about true love. Especially after the shit I've been through."

"How did you get away from your abusive baby father?" Kendrick was curious since Calista said he was violent toward her.

"Let's just say that my father handled it." Calista told him the truth without telling him the answer.

Kendrick knew precisely what that meant, but it wasn't his business to speak on. Calista made a turn to pull into the hospice building. Kendrick looked at the facility. It looked more like a fancy hospital to him. He wondered what it was like to have a mother on drugs. Was love still there? Were Calista and her mother on talking terms? He knew having a controlling mother was hard, so he could imagine how a mother with cancer could be.

They both got out of the car and walked into the building. Calista opened her mother's room door.

"Hey, Ma," Calista said, searching her mother's face for some expression.

"Calista, who is this?" Naomi asked, surprised.

"This is Kendrick, and he's the one who saved me when I got attacked." Calista prayed her mother didn't act like Kendrick's mother did.

"Young man, you better come over here and give me a hug for saving my daughter." Naomi stretched out her arms.

Kendrick wasted no time as he walked over and hugged Naomi. It felt good to be accepted. When Naomi hugged Kendrick, she could tell he was a good man. Calista sat on the bed and played with Amari. Amari crawled to the edge of the bed and reached out for Kendrick. This surprised Calista because her daughter had never done this. Usually, Amari was afraid or shy when it came to men. This came from seeing her father abuse her mother.

"Don't be afraid. You can pick her up." Calista's heart was filled with happiness.

"I'm not afraid. I just didn't want to offend any-one." Kendrick walked over and picked up the baby.

"She likes you," Calista said as she watched how Amari reacted toward Kendrick.

"I like her too." Kendrick kissed Amari on the cheek as she smiled, revealing her dimples.

Naomi sat in the chair smiling, glad to see a joyful moment. But her smile slowly faded when she heard Freeway's voice in the back of her head saying, *"When are you going to tell your daughter?"* She knew time was not on her side. How do you tell your only child such a thing? She had no choice but to do it now. She signaled to get Calista's attention. Calista walked over.

"What's up? You okay?" She put her arm around her mother's thin shoulder.

"Yeah, but I need to talk to you," Naomi murmured.

"Mom, why are you whispering?" Calista removed her arm from around her mother.

"We need to talk alone. Please, it's important." Naomi dropped her head sadly.

"OK, Mom, hold up." She noticed that her mom's whole mood had changed.

Calista had no idea what was happening, but she knew something was up. She walked over and asked Kendrick if he could step out and play with Amari in the hallway. Kendrick made sure that she was OK with him taking her daughter out of the room. She nodded in approval, kissed him on the cheek, and closed the door behind him.

"Mom, what's the big idea? I thought you liked Kendrick," Calista questioned with her arms folded.

"This not about Kendrick, baby." Naomi couldn't even look up at her daughter.

"Then what's this about?"

"Calista, you have to promise you won't hate me."

"Mom, you need to hurry up because it's rude to have him sitting in the hallway like that."

"I know, I know, but I need to get this off my chest before it's too late."

"Mom, just spit it out. Damn!"

"I'm dying from ovarian cancer, Calista, and it's caused by my years of drug usage. It's all my fault."

Calista stood there and said nothing. The silence had her mother scared. Naomi could deal with it if her daughter yelled, but the silent treatment was killing her. Instead, Calista just looked at her mom with a stoic look. Then tears began to roll down her cheeks. She turned around, snatched the door open, and left her mom in a lonely, cold, and very quiet room.

"Let's go, Kendrick."

"Let me say goodbye to your mom."

"Kendrick, fuck that. Let's go."

Just that quick, Kendrick knew something had gone wrong in that room. He didn't know about their conversation, but it must have been intense. Calista was already in the car when he got to the parking lot. He put Amari in the backseat and buckled her in safely. Before he could even open his door, Calista started the car and revved the engine. Kendrick knew he had to calm her down, and he had to do it now. He was not about to let her drive in this condition with a baby in the backseat.

"Look, you need to calm down and tell me what's going on—right now," pressed Kendrick. "I can drive if need be," he offered.

Calista shot him a grimacing stare.

"You wouldn't understand." She put the car in reverse.

"Calista, don't drive this damn car with your baby in here while you're angry."

"You don't fucking understand." She started punching the steering wheel.

"Baby, I got you. What's up?" He reached over to hug her, but first, he put the car in park. Then he wrapped both arms around her.

As her tears fell on his shoulder, he wondered what the hell happened when that door closed behind him. At this moment, he felt his only job was to comfort her and get her mind right. She moved from under him and looked in the backseat at Amari's pretty eyes. She felt bad about breaking down in front of her daughter. She thought Amari had already seen too much.

"My mother is dying." Calista's voice was soft and broken.

"Say what? Why are you acting like you didn't know this?"

"Because I didn't, Kendrick. I fucking didn't! My mom hid it from me. I just thought she was doing chemo," she explained.

"I don't understand." He couldn't fathom how she didn't know her mother was dying.

"My mother is dying from cancer. It's spreading, and she never told me."

"What did you say when she told you?" he pressed.

"Nothing. I just left." Calista calmly put the car in drive and pulled off.

"Where are we going?" He was worried about Calista's mental state at that moment. Hearing that your mom is dying from cancer is a hard blow for anybody to take, he thought.

"My house," she answered.

"Wait, you have a house?"

"Yeah, my father bought it for me. I haven't even seen the inside yet."

"The same father you just met?"

If Kendrick had to guess, he would have to say that Calista's father was beyond rich to buy her a house as soon as she arrived in Atlanta. He could relate to her about missing fathers because he had never met his.

Kendrick was still shocked that Calista had run out of her mother's room without saying anything about her dying. But then again, what do you say to news like that? Besides, it was hidden from her, so it was a sudden shock. He figured her mom had the disease for a long time and used crack to self-medicate. A moment flashed through Kendrick's head about calling his mother, but he instantly dismissed it.

Calista finally pulled up to her house.

"Can you get Amari for me? I think she fell asleep."

"Yeah, no problem," Kendrick agreed. He just wanted Calista in a good headspace.

"As I said, I haven't been in my house yet, so I don't know what it looks like. Shit, it probably don't even have any furniture," she giggled.

Kendrick leaned over and kissed her. He was just so happy to see her smile again. He gently rubbed her cheek, and they both felt butterflies surrounding their energy. They kissed once more, then got out of the car. Kendrick picked up Amari while Calista unlocked the door to her new home.

When she opened the door . . . she was met with shock. The home was beautiful and had a color scheme of black-and-white furniture. She walked through the house, admiring every room. Kendrick was also amazed when he walked in. He put Amari in one of the bedrooms since she was still asleep.

Calista wanted to call her father so badly, but he said emergencies only. The hardwood floors shined like they had been hand polished. Beautiful paintings accented the pastel-colored walls. The high ceilings gave the interior a majestic look. Calista's eyes widened at the beautifully decorated house.

After separately examining the home, they met back in the living room, where Calista hugged Kendrick. As they locked eyes, she felt a burning desire in her heart. So, she grabbed his face and passionately tongue-kissed him. Kendrick's dick began to grow, pressing against the seam of his zipper. Calista unzipped his pants, pulled out his manhood, and stroked it. Next, Kendrick ripped open her shirt and sucked on her breast. His tongue played with her nipple.

"Oh shit," she cooed.

"Fuck, I want this like yesterday," he said.

Calista's pussy was soaking wet when Kendrick finally ran his hand under her skirt.

"Oh fuck. That's it. Stroke my clit," she moaned.

He pulled up her skirt. Her legs rested on his shoulders as her ass hung off the sofa.

"You must have known I was going to be eating this pussy today," he joked as he looked into her eyes while rolling her clit between his fingers.

Fighting to keep her eyes open as shudders of ecstasy ran through her body, she moaned,

"Eat this pussy, Kendrick." Kendrick opened the folds of her pussy. Then he licked around her throbbing clit as he eased two fingers in and out of her sopping wet pussy. Calista moaned in ecstasy as Kendrick's tongue slurped, sucked, and licked her throbbing pussy. Her legs suddenly shook uncontrollably as he sucked her clit, then slid a finger in her ass and pussy with light, circular motions.

She tightened her grip on his head as she cried, "Oh shiit. I'm coming, Kendrick. It won't stop."

Kendrick kept feasting on her pussy, even after his face was coated with her juices. Calista's body convulsed as he finally stopped eating her love box. Gently, he eased his fingers out of her orifices and sat back, smiling. She was still slightly convulsing even after he stopped.

"You ready for me to beat up this pussy?" he smiled as he wiped her love juices off his face.

A winded Calista stuttered, "Yes, long strokes, please." Calista was moaning and screaming so loudly that she had to cover her mouth.

He stood up, his dick like the Eiffel Tower, straight and leaning slightly. He picked her up as she wrapped her legs around his waist. She pushed his dick inside her as she screamed out and came instantly. She was grinding as she bounced on his long, curved dick, and he pounded her. With every stroke, she begged him never to leave. Kendrick nibbled on her neck while he went deeper. She was so wet and warm. Finally, he exploded inside her, screaming that he loved her.

After they both climaxed, they collapsed on the living room floor. They definitely had just reached cloud nine. They lay in the middle of the living room floor, naked, holding each other.

"I want you as my girl," he said as he gently kissed the back of her head as he held her.

"You got me, boo. I'm not going nowhere. You got me drifting on a cloud I never want to come down from."

Even though Calista felt like she was in orgasmic bliss, she knew she had to go back and face her mother and deal with a pain she wished she could just ignore. However, right now, she was going to live in her blissful moment.

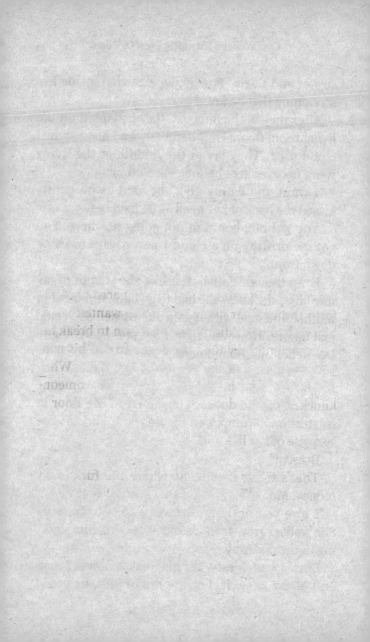

Chapter 26

Choices

After not hearing from her son for twenty-four hours, Mona began to worry as she paced back and forth through her living room. She wanted to call him so badly but didn't want her son to break her heart again. Every time she began to dial his number, she'd stop as she got to the last digit. When she finally built up the courage to call, someone knocked on the door. She headed to the door in frustration, swung open the door . . . and got the surprise of her life.

"Brasco!"

"That's right; it's me. So where the fuck is my money, Mona?"

"I owe you nothing, Brasco, and you know it." She walked away from the door, leaving him standing in the doorway.

Brasco was shiesty, but his weak spot was Mona, and Mona knew it. For the life of him, he could never shake her out of his life, even when he told her to go on with her life when he did a seventeen-year sentence. He refused to expect her to do his bid with him.

Brasco was tall, bearded, had dark skin, and his body was like a continued tattoo. His dreadlocks were braided up, and his face was babysitting high cheekbones and deep dimples. Brasco made it his priority always to keep tabs on Mona. He sat beside her.

"Did I tell you to come inside my house?" Mona rolled her eyes.

"Really, Mona, I'm the one who paid for this fucking house," he smirked.

"Brasco, do you realize how much money you *owe* me for raising a son that you abandoned? Nigga, please," she spat.

"You know damn well I didn't abandon him." He became furious when Mona kept saying that.

"What do you call going to jail and leaving us, nigga?"

"You knew what I was doing when you met me. So don't act like my lifestyle was a surprise."

"No. *My* surprise was when I moved here and found out you were running shit heavy and had no plans to find us." Mona crossed her legs with an attitude.

"You told me to stay away—remember?"

"Since when have you listened to me, Brasco? Did you listen when I told your ass to leave them streets alone when we were young?"

"No, I didn't. So how is he anyway?"

"Just like you—stubborn as ever and still loves those games."

"He still at the top of his class?"

"How the hell did you know that shit, Brasco?" Mona turned and looked at him, shocked that he knew something about their son.

"I told you I kept a close ear on him when I could."

"I told him that his father died. You do realize if he finds out about you, he may never forgive me because of that lie?"

"I understand, Mona. You want things to stay the same."

"I don't *want* things to stay the same; they *have* to stay the same."

Brasco didn't like Mona's attitude about the whole situation. No matter what he said or did, she would not budge, even after all the money he spent on her. He knew it was his fault because of the life he chose to live, but he wanted to know his son now. This was a grave he dug for himself. He was a fool to think his money would change things.

"You really need to reconsider and let me see my son." He stood up.

"I told you that's not a good idea, Brasco."

"Why the fuck not, Mona?" He punched the palm of his hand with his fist.

"What type of role model would you be for my son?" Mona didn't like Brasco's aggressive movement. Even though she didn't fear him, she knew how dangerous he could become if provoked.

"What? Because I live a street life, you don't think I got guidance advice?"

"Look, you need to leave before he comes home. This is a situation I'm not trying to explain." Mona walked to the front door and opened it. She pointed to the open space, motioning for him to leave.

"You know what? I will leave, but what you're doing is wrong, and you know it."

"Brasco, I appreciate the money you let me borrow, believe it or not."

"Whatever. Fuck the loan. You don't have to pay me back. You better hope those pastry shops you got do well and never go out of business because, if they do, don't you fucking call me."

Mona watched Brasco walk out the door and, hopefully, out of her life for good. But deep down, she knew one thing. She knew if she were somebody else, Brasco probably would have killed her. Luckily, his heart belonged to her, which was heavy leverage on her part.

She slammed the door after he left and returned to where she left off before Brasco knocked on it. She was back building up the courage to call her son again.

She sat back on the couch and crossed her legs. Never in her life did she think her son would go against her for some girl. Then again, things between them were not always great. She turned on the television, hoping it would take her mind off her son. It did for a little while . . . until a commercial for a new video game came across the screen, which made her immediately think of him. She shook her head as tears streamed from her eyes.

Nothing in this world could move her enough to make her emotional besides her son. Mona had always been a tough cookie, but her son was her heart, no matter what they went through. If anybody could break her spirit, it was definitely Kendrick. She named him that for a reason. She knew he would have unique gifts and talents. All she ever wanted was for him to survive and be successful. No matter what, she loved her son.

"Fuck it." She dialed his number.

Calista stepped out of the shower, and Kendrick was right there to meet her with a towel. He dried her off as he kissed her forehead. Like always, her heart began to melt. She kissed him gently on the lips.

"Where's Amari, boo?"

"She's sitting on a blanket in the living room playing."

"Please, go sit with her while I get dressed."
Calista wanted to call her father, but she needed to
be alone.

"Sure, no problem, but hurry, my Queen."

"I got you, boo."

Kendrick kissed her once more and headed
downstairs. Calista quickly threw on her clothes,
grabbed her phone, and called her father. He
didn't pick up. It went to voicemail. She had to
know if he knew that her mother was dying. She
called again. Fuck his emergency rule, she thought
to herself. Her foot was impatiently tapping as the
phone rang.

"Calista, this better be important," Freeway
demanded.

"Oh, this is important. So, did you know?"

"Know what, Calista?" He was already growing
impatient.

"Did you know that my mother was dying? Don't
lie to me."

"First, I don't fear anybody enough to part my
lips to lie. Second, watch who you're talking to like
that. Of course, I knew she was dying. Who do you
think made her tell you?"

"Don't you two think you kept enough secrets
from me? My whole life's been a damn lie." She
began to cry.

"Calista, you listen to me. Put on your big girl
panties and handle this. I'll call you later." Freeway
hung up.

Just like a whisper in the wind, her father was gone. On the one hand, she hated what he did, but on the other hand, he was blunt and pushed her to be strong. She slid her phone into her bra and headed downstairs to join her daughter and Kendrick. When she reached the bottom step, Kendrick immediately sensed something was wrong. In his mind, he felt she finally spoke with her mother.

"So, how did it go with your mother?"

"What makes you think I spoke with my mother?" she said, getting on the floor with Amari.

"Because, bae, you are in that mood again. I don't like to see you like this."

"No, it was my father this time."

"Oh, is everything OK?"

"Not really. He has no emotion or heart, but at the same time, he knew what to say to push me."

"Yeah, I feel you. My mom can be controlling, but she knows how to push the agenda for tough love."

"I think we need to smooth things over with our parents," Calista suggested.

Before Kendrick could reply, his phone rang. He reached into his pocket and noticed it was his mother. He wasn't ready to talk to her just yet, but he saw the look Calista had given him, so he answered anyway.

"Yeah, Ma?"

"Kendrick, please come home for at least an hour to talk," she pleaded.

"I was headed that way, but, Ma, I'm not staying long, so if you're going to be controlling and not willing to listen, then tell me now 'cause I'm not going to waste my time."

"I promise I'll listen, son."

"OK." Kendrick hung up. He could hear the sadness in his mom's voice.

Calista already had Amari and her things packed up and headed outside. This would not be a fun day for either of them, but things had to be repaired. What they *did* know was that no matter what anybody thought, they were going to be together.

When they got into the car, Calista didn't know why, but she felt like she had to do something just for safety since she was in a new city.

"Hey, I need to give you something just in case anything happens to me."

"Calista, nothing is going to happen to you. So what are you talking about?" Kendrick was concerned that she wasn't telling him something.

"Kendrick, don't argue with me about this. Just give me your phone." She put out her hand to receive his phone.

"Fine, but I can protect you, you know that," he said, giving her his phone.

"This is my dad's number. His name is Freeway. Only call him if something ever happens to me, you promise?" She programmed her dad's number and name into his phone.

"I'm pretty sure I'm not going to need to, Calista, but OK." After the number was stored, he took his phone and slid it back into his pocket.

They drove off, heading to Mona's house first. Kendrick didn't have much to say after the stunt Calista had just pulled. He felt like she didn't trust him enough to protect her. But Calista knew how powerful her dad was. They stopped at a gas station before getting to Mona's house.

Kendrick got out and pumped the gas while Calista went inside to pay for the fuel. She walked down the aisle to get some snacks for her daughter. While looking at some fruit snacks, she heard a familiar, scary voice.

"You remember me, little mama?" He grabbed her arm.

"Get the fuck off of me!" She snatched her arm away, turned around, and almost pissed on herself when she saw who it was.

"Yeah, the name's Jabo. You better remember the name. Your little boyfriend saved you the last time." His gold teeth shined through his threat.

"You better get the fuck out of my face."

Kendrick grabbed Amari and headed toward the store because he felt Calista was taking too long.

He opened the door and saw she was in a standoff with the same nigga he had beat up.

When Jabo saw Kendrick, he pushed Calista down and ran out of the store. Since Kendrick was holding Amari, he couldn't give chase, so he helped Calista up and asked if she was OK. Although she was a little shaken, she was unhurt, so they decided to continue with their plans.

After finally paying for the gas, they ended up at Mona's house. Kendrick didn't want to leave Calista, but she assured him she would be back in an hour. He kissed her, got out of the car, and watched as she drove away. He prayed that she would be okay by herself during this time. Then he walked into the house to have that conversation with his mother.

Chapter 27

Amends

When Kendrick entered the house, his mother jumped off the couch, ran, and hugged him. But he pushed her off.

Mona stood back and looked at her son with tears in her eyes. She felt as if a giant boulder had crushed her whole world. Kendrick sat on the couch, looked at his mom, and shook his head.

"You just don't want me to be happy, do you?"

"Why would you say that, son?" She sat beside him.

"You do *everything* to make me unhappy."

"No, I do not," she said in denial.

"Mom, please, when I was in school, you didn't want me to play any sports."

"I just didn't want you to get hurt, that's all."

"No, Ma. Let's be real. You wanted me all to yourself."

For the first time, Mona realized that her son was telling a hurtful truth. Only God knows what would happen if Kendrick discovered that she had lied about his father dying—and that he was still alive. And he was the one who gave her the money for the house and the pastry business.

His father had wanted to know him, and what did she do? Kicked him out. She felt weak with all the guilt overwhelming her.

"You didn't have to treat Calista like that. She did *nothing* for that disrespect."

"I just don't want you to get involved with the wrong woman and get hurt. She has a baby, so I know the father is lurking somewhere."

"Her baby father is dead, for your info."

"Kendrick, I didn't know that." Now, she felt embarrassed.

"Did you take the time to find out? No. Instead, you did like you always did and tried to control the situation."

"I only want you to make better choices and return to school. By the way, you have an upcoming college interview."

Kendrick's next statement was interrupted by a knock on the door. Mona had no idea who it could be since not many people knew where she lived. She didn't want to answer the door until she resolved her issues with her son. She could tell he was hurting. However, the knock got louder, so she hurried to the door and snatched it open.

"Fucking what?" Then she froze when she saw Brasco.

"Girl, miss me with that noise. I think my shades fell out of my pocket when I was here."

"You can't come in. I'm busy right now." She stood in the doorway to block his passage.

But Brasco walked right past her—and stopped in his tracks when he saw his son. Mona was so scared of what he might say. Suddenly, Brasco turned around and, smiling, looked at Mona. It felt so good to see his son. He walked over to Kendrick and stuck out his hand to greet his son.

"Damn, so this is your son, Kendrick." Brasco chose not to reveal that he was his father. Instead, he respected Mona's wishes . . . for now.

"Yes, do I know you?"

"Naw, little homie, but I was the one that gave your mom the money to start the business."

"Look, we'll pay you back as soon as we can. We don't want no trouble." Kendrick stood up to protect his mom if he had to.

"It's all good. She paid me." Looking around, Brasco spotted his glasses, grabbed them, and walked toward the door.

"OK, I'll see you around," Mona said nervously as she walked him to the door.

"You owe me," he whispered in Mona's ear as he left.

It was a huge relief to Mona that he didn't reveal who he really was, but when she turned around, she saw the stern look on her son's face. She didn't know what to expect from him. She had no idea if he could see the resemblance to his father.

"Mom, don't borrow any more money." Kendrick sat back down.

"I won't, honey." She was just happy he said nothing else about Brasco.

"I think you owe Calista an apology, Ma."

"Why?"

"What do you mean, 'why'?" Kendrick felt like his mom hadn't listened to a word he had said.

"It's not like I am going to see her again."

"Actually, Calista and I are a couple now."

"Kendrick, what? How—when?" She was shocked.

"It's hard to explain, but our energy just clicked somehow."

In reality, she knew exactly what he meant. She and Brasco had that same energy when they first met. But somehow, they grew apart once he had got locked up. She never knew she would have to deal with an intense inferno of energy again. There was no way she could argue with what he felt. If her son was truly in love and got hit by Cupid this hard, no way could she fight it. She knew because of the way she loved Brasco. Nobody could come between them . . . until he went to prison.

"Son, if she means this much to you, I *will* apologize, but let me ask you one question first."

"Go ahead; I'm listening." He was waiting.

"Did you meet her mother?"

"I did, and we hugged and everything, but, Ma, she's dying from cancer."

Just like that, Mona felt sorry for Calista and how she treated her. No child, little or grown, should have to experience such deep pain. She couldn't imagine what that girl must be feeling.

"Kendrick, I will certainly apologize to her. I promise."

"Good. She's coming back within the hour to get me, so you can do it then. Ma, don't let me down. She means a lot to me."

Calista walked down the hall to her mother's room, holding Amari. However, once in the room, she didn't see her mother anywhere. She sat on the bed, thinking she was at one of the drug meetings she had to attend. This gave her time to prepare what she would say to a dying mother. Calista felt like she was selfish because her mother was the one dying.

However, after an hour passed, she went to the front desk to see why her mom's meeting was so long.

"Excuse me. I'm trying to find my mother, Naomi. She's not in her room," she said to the receptionist.

"Oh my, baby, your mother was coughing up blood and was taken to the hospital."

"Say what? And you didn't notify anybody?"

"Actually, we did. We called a Mr. Freeway."

"That's my father. Can I have directions to the hospital, please?"

The lady behind the desk wasted no time writing down the directions to the hospital. Then Calista ran out of the building like a hot bullet shot out of the chamber. She got to her car, quickly strapped Amari into her baby seat, and typed the address in the GPS on her phone. A moment later, she was on her way. She definitely was now feeling all types of guilt from not talking to her mother. Suddenly, a question popped up in her mind. Why hadn't her father called her?

She zoomed down the highway. God must have been on her side because as fast as she was driving, no cop spotted her, and she caught all the green lights. She knew she shouldn't be going like that, especially with her baby in the car, but her mother was dying with every second she was wasting. Finally, she got to the hospital, quickly parked, grabbed Amari, and ran into the lobby. The first person she saw was her father. He was stunned to see her. He stopped her right where she stood.

"What are you doing here?"

"What do you mean? My mother is here."

"Calista, you really shouldn't see her like this."

He gently took her arm and escorted her to the nearest seat. She feared for the worst. Had her mother already passed away? Was it too late for her to say goodbye? She was crying uncontrollably. Freeway had his associate take the baby out of Calista's arms. Freeway knew he had to play father to his grieving daughter. He wrapped his arms around her and told her it would be OK.

"It's far worse than we thought. I didn't even know she had all this going on."

"Dad, what's wrong with her? Please tell me."

Freeway realized his daughter had called him "dad" for the first time. He had never felt more sensitive in his life than right now. He kissed her on the forehead and knew it was the love he'd been missing all his life. He'd been looking for this to fill the void in his life. He always thought it was a love for a woman. Instead, it was the love of his daughter, and he wanted to protect her, but not even he could fight this tragedy his daughter was going through.

"Look at me, Calista. Your mother is near her end. The doctor doesn't think she'll make it through the night."

"No!" Calista fell out of the seat to her knees, crying.

"I can take you to her room, but, baby, you can't see her like this. You've got to be strong, you hear me?" He wiped away her tears.

Freeway's associate was surprised. He'd never before seen this side of his boss. Of course, he didn't expect that Freeway had a soft side after all the blood he had spilled on the streets.

This was the very reason Freeway left his daughter and her mother. He never wanted anybody to use this love against him in the streets. He picked up his daughter from the floor and sat her back in the chair. After drying her tears, Freeway showed her where her mother's room was and allowed her to go alone.

As soon as Calista stepped into the room, she heard all the beeping from the machines that were hooked up to her mother. She wanted to break down and cry but knew she couldn't. She wanted to bawl with every step she took to her mother's bed.

She sat in the chair next to her mother's bed and held her hand. Naomi's hand still felt so soft and warm. She could still feel her mother's love just by touching her hand. She looked at her mother and lay her head on the bed. Next, she felt a soft hand running through her hair. She looked up. Her mom was smiling at her but not speaking. Then softly, she heard her mother's beautiful voice.

"Baby, don't cry. It's OK. You're a big girl."

"Mom, I'm so sorry." Calista couldn't help it. She began to cry.

"Sorry for what, honey? I lived my life and chose to put drugs in my body all those years. Now, I'm paying for the choices I made. After using drugs for so long, I found out that many of them were mixed with cancer-causing cutting agents."

Calista had to admit even though her mom did drugs, she still did a hell of a job raising her. She never abandoned her motherly duties, not once. Her mama kept her in fancy clothes, and she ate well every night.

"Mom, why didn't you tell me?"

"Baby, you had your own life to deal with."

"So what? You're my mother."

"I know, Calista. I just wanted you not to blame your father for leaving and for you to get close to him. Believe it or not, he's a loving man. He just didn't want the life he chose to live to affect you negatively."

As Calista thought about it, her father did show her love when she broke down in the lobby. Her father may have been ruthless, but he loved her. Instantly, Calista jumped up when she heard the machine flatline.

"Mommy, no!"

Freeway rushed into the room and realized the mother of his daughter had just left to be with God.

Chapter 28

Choices

Kendrick kept calling and calling Calista's phone, but he got no answer. He began to worry. Mona noticed his anxiety. She really hoped this girl was not messing around on him.

Kendrick was hoping that the guy he beat up hadn't caught up to his girl. So he called once more—still no answer.

"Son, you said she went to see her mother, right?"

"Yeah."

"Well, she's probably talking to her mom and can't hear the phone." She tried to calm him.

Mona knew even though her son was an intelligent man and went to college, he still had street in him. After all, he was his father's son. In many ways, Kendrick was just like Brasco, only he stayed out of the street and went to school. Mona knew her son was not to be played with. So she walked over and rubbed his shoulders.

"Mom, I need your car."

"Kendrick, I can't have you going out and getting into trouble."

"Ma, either give me your car, or I'll call a taxi. Either way, I'm going." Kendrick was determined to find out where Calista was.

"Fine, but please, call me in an hour." She pointed to the table where her keys were.

Kendrick kissed his mom, ran to the table, and snatched the keys. Mona appreciated that at least she got a kiss this time when he left.

Kendrick walked out, prepared for anything. He jumped into the car and sped off, wasting no time getting to the hospice facility. Quickly, he jumped out of the car, searching for Calista's vehicle—but he had no luck, so he went inside and asked the receptionist where she and her mom were. The receptionist told him what had happened and gave him the hospital's address.

Kendrick raced to the hospital. He couldn't believe that his girl's mom could be dying at this very moment. He had to get there to be her support. He knew that she probably didn't have anybody else at this dark hour in her life.

He got to the hospital in record time, and as he rushed through the front door, he saw Calista crying and some man with his arms around her. Kendrick lost control. He wanted to be the only one to comfort her. So he ran over and pushed the guy off Calista.

"Get your fucking hands off my girl, mother-fucker," he growled.

Kendrick had no clue who he had just put his hands on.

"Boy, who the fuck are you?" Freeway grabbed Kendrick by the throat and tossed him across the hospital floor.

Calista tried to stop her dad, but he was far too strong and powerful. He moved her out of the way and started to kick Kendrick in the stomach so many times that he coughed up blood. Calista finally got control of her dad and begged him to stop.

"Dad, no. Please, stop. That's my boyfriend!"

"Your boyfriend? Well, this nigga's about to be in a coffin."

"Dad, please, let me handle it."

"Get him the fuck out of here before I kill him. What the fuck y'all looking at?" Freeway snapped at the crowd in the lobby, looking on in shock.

Calista went to Kendrick's side and helped him up. Then she walked him outside. She hated to admit it, but Kendrick brought this on himself. He just wasn't ready for the ass whooping that came with these troubles.

When they got outside, he jerked away from her. She couldn't believe that he was mad at *her* now. Calista tried to wipe the blood from his lip when he sat on a bench, but he refused her.

"Get the fuck off of me!" He pushed her away.

"*Really?* You coming at me like this?" She sighed heavily.

"You let that nigga put his hands on me."

"That's my father, and my father don't play that shit. Kendrick, you don't want those troubles."

"I don't give a fuck who he is. Why couldn't you call me?"

"Because my mother was dying, and I was in a panic."

"You couldn't even answer the phone when I called." Then angrily, he wiped the blood from his mouth.

"You sound very selfish right now. My mother is dead, and you rushed in here and put *your* hands on *my* dad. You're lucky he didn't kill your ass," barked Calista. Now, *she* was mad.

"Seems like you don't fucking need me here," he frowned.

"Kendrick, if you're going to act this way, you need to leave. You're acting like an insecure bitch," she said.

"*This* the way you're going to flex on me right fucking now?" Kendrick stood up, fussing.

Freeway came out of the door, still angry that this young-ass clown put his hands on him, and on top of that, he was now yelling at his daughter. When Calista saw her father, she quickly stepped in front of him to let him know she had things under control. Then she turned and yelled at Kendrick, telling him to leave.

"If I pull out of this parking lot, I'm *not* coming back."

"Boy, if you don't get the fuck out of here, I'll put some hot shit in you right now," Freeway spat with his 9 mm in his hand. "I done had plenty mammies crying over you little motherfuckers," he barked.

Kendrick looked at Calista, rolled his eyes, walked his bruised body to his mother's car, and drove off. Freeway looked at his daughter with nothing but disapproval.

"What the fuck is wrong with you?" he snapped. "What?" she answered.

"Don't 'what' me. Your mother is dead, and I'm out here dealing with this bullshit. I can't believe you're entertaining a clown," he frowned.

"How was I supposed to know he would show up here?" Calista couldn't believe *she* was getting blamed for this.

"Nobody puts their hands on me. Now, I got to kill him."

"Dad, no! It's over, OK? He's gone. I'll handle it later, I promise."

"You better because if I got to, it's not going to be pretty, and you gon' be burying another nigga."

Kendrick zoomed down the road, wondering how the hell Calista could play him for her long-lost father, whom she had just met. But then again, they just met as well. He was holding his side with one hand and steering with the other. Pain shot up his left side. He did a quick U-turn when he realized he had passed Brasco's Bar. He damn sure could use a drink right about now.

He pulled into the parking lot, and when he put the car in park, he felt all the pain from the licking that Freeway had given him. It took all his strength to open the door.

Still angry, he walked in, sat, and banged on the table for the bartender. All the patrons were staring at him. He didn't give a damn, though. He just wanted a drink. The bartender casually walked over to him.

"So, what you having since you're in a rush?"

"I'll tell you like this. Tonight *isn't* the night to fuck with me," warned Kendrick.

"I don't have to serve you, so you can get the fuck out," threatened the bartender.

Before Kendrick could think about jumping across the counter and dragging out the disrespect-ful-ass bartender, a hand touched his shoulder. He looked behind him and saw Brasco looking him dead in the face.

In Kendrick's mind, he was about to be escorted out.

"I didn't do nothing. But he's acting like he owns this bitch," spat Kendrick.

"Is that how you fucking talk to customers?" Brasco stared at the bartender with a stoic expression.

"No, boss." Fear came over him.

"Let me talk to you in the back right quick."

He told Kendrick to sit tight as he and the nervous bartender walked to the back office.

"What's up, boss man?" the bartender asked.

"I know you're new here, but that's my family," frowned Brasco.

Brasco walked into the office and sat on the edge of his desk. The bartender closed the door slowly behind him, so nervous that he was ready to pee on himself.

"Have you lost your damn mind?"

"No, sir."

"No, I think you have."

"Brasco, please, I apologize."

Brasco jumped off his desk, grabbed him by the back of his collar, and slammed him down on the desk face-first, busting his nose and lip and cracking a few teeth. He tried to move from Brasco's grip, but it was impossible. Brasco was not about to let this fool disrespect his son.

Next, Brasco threw him on the floor, opened the desk drawer, and pulled out a 9 mm. He screwed on a silencer and stuck it to the bartender's head.

"What if I end your life right now, bitch?"

"Please, Brasco, I'll go and apologize."

"Too late." Brasco pulled the trigger, sending a quiet bullet to the back of his head.

After that, Brasco left the office, walked over to his head security, who was actually his hitta, and whispered in his ear. His hitta went straight to the back. Kendrick was no fool. He knew what that was all about. Then Brasco went behind the bar and poured Kendrick and him a drink.

"That guy isn't coming back, is he?"

"No, he left. This job wasn't for him," Brasco lied.

"Your mom know you in the bar at this time of night?" Brasco finished his drink in one gulp.

"Shit, I'm grown," growled Kendrick.

"You may be grown, but your momma crazy about your ass too."

"Yeah, I know. I'm not usually out like this, but my girl and I got into it tonight. I was wilding, and some shit popped off," frowned Kendrick.

"I see. Is that why you're holding your ribs?"

"Yeah, I went to the hospital looking for her 'cause her mom was sick. When I got there, I thought her dad was some nigga she was messing with . . . and, well, he fucked me up, I have to admit. By the way, her mom died."

Brasco didn't care about the last part his son said. He was only focused on somebody putting their hands on his flesh and blood. Brasco poured another drink and slammed his shot glass on the table.

"Let's go straighten this shit out," ordered Brasco.

"Where we going?" Kendrick finished off his drink.

"We going to the hospital and pay this nigga a visit."

"I don't think that's a good idea. This guy is pretty heavy-duty in the streets, I think. I'm pretty sure he's an OG in the game."

"Boy, if you don't get your ass up and let's go . . ." ordered Brasco. Kendrick dropped his head and followed him out of the bar.

They drove separate cars and went to the hospital. Kendrick was nervous about returning after what Calista's father did to him, but he could tell that Brasco was no bitch either. They got to the hospital, and Calista was in the parking lot by her car. They pulled up alongside her. Brasco jumped out of the car first. Kendrick slowly opened his car door to ease out since he was still in pain.

"Is that your girlfriend?" Brasco yelled.

Kendrick nodded.

"What's this about?" Calista questioned.

"So, you went to get somebody to fight my daddy for you?" she fumed.

Kendrick dropped his head in embarrassment.

"Damn, you're a bitch," she sighed.

"Kill all the bullshit," Brasco snapped.

"Where the fuck is your daddy, girl?" Brasco was in a rage now.

"He's coming out of the hospital." Calista put Amari inside the car.

Freeway was making his way across the parking lot. Brasco couldn't make out his face, but he was already cussing toward Freeway, saying he was about to beat his ass. When Freeway stepped into the light from the light post that shined above their heads, Brasco saw who he was facing—and froze.

"Nigga, you talking to me? Yeah, I whooped the little nigga's ass. You want some?" barked Freeway.

Brasco's words caught in his throat. He had no idea that his son was talking about Freeway. Brasco knew he had no dogs in the fight against Freeway. Freeway told Calista to get in her car and pull off, which she did. "Nigga, I asked you a question. You know who the fuck I am. Don't play with me."

Brasco began to stutter, which pissed off Freeway. He pulled out his gun, stuck it to Brasco's head, cocked and loaded. All Brasco could think about was what the fuck he had gotten himself into.

Chapter 29

Dying Flame

Calista was driving home, but her father was heavy on her mind. She knew her dad only revealed himself to help because he knew her mom was dying. She refused to let her flesh and blood get in trouble because her boyfriend couldn't take an ass whooping and, like a bitch, went to get help. She turned her car around to make sure her father was good.

When she returned to the hospital, she saw her father had his gun drawn on the guy who had approached them earlier. Calista jumped out and yelled for her dad's associate, Shy. She made the associate watch her baby while trying to defuse this situation before it went too far. Kendrick was standing there holding his side, looking scared as hell.

"Dad, no! Put your gun away."

"No, this nigga bad enough to approach me, so he must want to go see God personally."

"Dad, look at me. Let this stupid man go."

Freeway wanted to put a bullet in his head so badly for disrespecting him and who he was.

Brasco was doing something that he never thought he'd do—pleading for his life. It was so ironic how he just took a life at his bar like a badass, but now, he was the one being a bitch along with Kendrick. Had he known what he was facing, he would have stayed put. Freeway smacked Brasco in the face with the butt of his gun, then threw him to the ground.

"If my daughter wasn't here, both of you lame sons of bitches would be dead." Freeway signaled to his associate so he could leave.

"Dad, thank you. I owe you."

"Now, you see why I couldn't be in your life—because motherfuckers like *that* want to test me." Freeway was beyond pissed. He got in his car with his associate and drove off.

Calista looked at Kendrick and Brasco and just shook her head. They had no idea what they were up against. Brasco said nothing. He was too embarrassed that he couldn't defend his son. So instead, he just got in his car and drove off.

Calista went to the car to make sure her baby was still sleeping, and sure enough, she was sound asleep through all the commotion. She smiled at her baby, thinking her little girl could sleep through a storm. She knew she had to confront Kendrick for the bullshit he pulled. She stormed back in his direction.

"What the fuck, nigga?" She slapped him.

"What the fuck you hit me for?"

"*You* caused this. I love you, Kendrick, but you almost made my father take a man's life."

"You know what, Calista? You sure suddenly got a lot of love for a father you just met." He felt betrayed.

"No matter how long he's been gone, he's my damn father and a man that doesn't mind taking a life."

"So, now, I mean nothing to you?" He felt hurt.

"I love you, but I will not choose between you and my father. At the end of the day, you're my man, but he will *always* be my father."

"Maybe there's not enough room in your life for your father *and* me." Kendrick couldn't believe he had just uttered those words.

"Well, if that's how you *really* feel, Kendrick." She crossed her arms and rolled her eyes.

"So, you choose your father over me? A man that can disappear out of your life at any moment?" Kendrick hoped Calista would choose their love over a father she had just met.

"I just got my father back, and I will *not* kick him to the curb, so, yes, I'm choosing my father."

Kendrick looked at Calista with hurtful eyes.
Finally, he realized that her choice was final. He
walked past her to get in his car. He started the car
and drove off slowly, hoping she would stop him.

Tears fell from her eyes as Kendrick drove away.
Her whole world was crumbling. Why did she have
to choose between him and her father? She took a
slow walk back to her car. The night air felt so cruel
to her. She got in her car and stuck the key in the
ignition.

Then she turned on the radio. Unfortunately, it
seemed like all they were playing were love songs.
She was not in the mood to listen to the shit she
was hearing, so she slowly drove back to her house.
She rolled the window down because she wanted
to feel the night air.

Amid all the bullshit, her mind constantly re-
minded her that she had lost her mother tonight.
Her tears were streaming because she had lost
Kendrick *and* her mother on the same night.

She pulled up to the curb next to her house, put
the car in park, and began punching the steering
wheel. She had so much anger and nowhere to
channel it. Finally, she reached into the back and
unbuckled Amari. Her baby was still asleep, even
snoring.

She walked into a cold, empty house. She and
Kendrick made a lot of sweet memories in the
place, which didn't make her feel any better. She

was too tired and exhausted to walk upstairs, so she laid Amari on the couch and curled up in a ball on the cold, carpeted floor. Today was a day she would never forget. This was like a complete nightmare for her that she couldn't wake up from.

Just when she thought that she had found happiness in all facets of her life . . . She lost it all in one single night. Why was her life so cursed? She loved Kendrick so much that she still could feel his energy all over her body, especially her heart.

Kendrick was driving like a maniac. He had to remind himself that he was driving his mother's car, not his own. What was he going to do now? He just lost the only woman that he genuinely loved. He pulled into his mom's driveway. Like usual, she was on the porch, waiting for him.

"Where the fuck you been?" She was yelling as she approached her car.

"Mom, not tonight." Kendrick felt weak from pain and heartache.

"What do you mean, 'not tonight'? Do you realize how long you've been gone?"

"Look, Ma, please, just go inside the house and leave me alone."

"Kendrick, something is going on, and you need to tell me right now."

Mona noticed how he was holding his ribs and was in pain. She opened the car door to get a full view of her son.

Her eyes grew big when she saw his busted lip. She went to touch his face, but he smacked her hand away. Then finally, he got out of the car and walked into the house. Mona walked behind him, worried.

"Kendrick, you better tell me what happened."

As he walked into the house, Brasco pulled up. Mona turned around to see what the hell he wanted. Brasco jumped from the car, ready to explain the whole situation, thinking that Kendrick had already told his mom what had gone down. Brasco told Mona everything, the entire story.

"Nigga, you did *what?*"

"I had no idea that it would be Freeway." He tried to explain the power that Freeway had.

"Look, I don't even know who that is, but you're trying to tell me that Kendrick's girlfriend's father is a fucking kingpin?"

"Actually, he's bigger than that. He has *everybody* in his pocket, including judges."

"You mean to tell me this man can move around and sell drugs and not be challenged by anybody?"

"That's the thing. He doesn't sell drugs anymore. He has multimillion-dollar businesses."

"I don't care who he is. He shouldn't have put his hands on my son." Mona couldn't believe one man could have so much power.

"I'm sorry, Mona." He knew she was pissed. Her son was everything to her.

"I don't know how, but you better fix this. This man put his hands on our son. I know there's a way you can make him realize that he can be touched too. Brasco, man the fuck up. You got power in this city, so use it for once." Mona walked off, leaving Brasco to his thoughts.

Brasco knew Mona was right. He did have power, but he knew he still couldn't measure up to Freeway. Nobody could. This man put in serious work in the streets. He did things that Brasco knew he could never do. Freeway was known as the man with no heart because he was so ruthless. Brasco knew he had to do something to redeem himself, and he had to do it fast. He jumped into his car, called his head hitta to put his plan in motion, and drove off, leaving Mona's house.

Mona saw her son sitting at the kitchen table when she walked into the house. At that moment, she didn't want to say anything. She knew he was hurting. She was afraid that something like that would happen, and she didn't want him to feel that heartbreak. She walked over, kissed him on the forehead, and let him be. With that type of pain, nothing could fix it, but time. So, she went to her room and left him to himself.

Kendrick sat at the table, feeling Calista's energy all over his heart. After sitting alone, he realized he was selfish. The girl's mom had just died. There was no other pain greater than that. Even though his mom got on his nerves and was controlling, he would be devastated if she died. He searched his mind over and over for how to fix things. How could he live with this empty feeling in his heart? It was like his soul was hungry for her; his spirit was starving for her spirit.

There was no doubt they had deep chemistry in a short time. Yet, all he could think of was why God would give him the perfect woman, then take her away. It was a knife to his soul.

"Son . . ." Mona couldn't help herself. She had to say something because her son was hurting.

"I'm not arguing with you." He spoke softly because of his pain.

"I didn't come to argue."

"OK, what's up?"

"You do know that time heals all things, right?" She took a seat at the table with him, holding his hand.

"I know, but this pain is too great to bear."

"I understand that, but I promise you'll make it through."

"Maybe I should just go back and focus on school."

"At this moment, you just need to take it easy and heal."

"Yeah, I guess so." Kendrick got up from the table.

"Where you going?" Mona was hoping he wasn't going out to find that girl.

"Just going outside to get some fresh air."

"You promise not to go anywhere?"

"Yeah, Ma, I promise."

Kendrick walked outside and sat on the porch. He looked up at the moon and the stars and wished he was the sky. He would be a blanket over the earth. The sky had no worries. Tears fell from his eyes. He never thought he would love a woman so much. He promised himself he would never fall in love, but it happened. How was he going to find a solution for this void . . . and was it even possible?

Kendrick stretched out on the porch, letting the universe talk to him. Then suddenly, he jumped up as a thought hit him. He'd be damned if he was going to let their love die.

Chapter 30

Sticky Situation

Brasco pulled up to a clothing store he owned. He was looking around for his head hitta, who he had called. He was getting frustrated because there was no time to waste. He put his car in park when he saw Jabo walking his way. He rolled down his window. Jabo was smoking on a blunt when he walked up to Brasco's car.

"Get in and put out that shit. You know I don't allow that shit in my car." He rolled up his window again.

"Sure thing, boss." Jabo walked around and got into the car.

"We got a fucking problem." Brasco began to explain.

"You the man, boss. You know I'll handle it."

"It's not that simple."

"I don't understand. You run the city, right?"

"Freeway is back in town."

"What? The legendary Freeway?"

"Yeah, and I had a run-in with his daughter."

"Oh, damn, so, what's up?"

"He put his hands on my son; I just can't let that fly."

Brasco began to run down the whole story about what happened. Finally, Jabo realized the people he was describing sounded a lot like who he was dealing with. Then Jabo began to tell his story and his falling out with Kendrick and Calista. Brasco looked at Jabo with an evil eye.

"Wait—so the guy you got into it with was at the pastry shop? Was he the owner?"

"Yeah, and I was going to shoot that nigga, but I didn't have my gun."

"Motherfucker, that's my *son*." Brasco reached over, grabbed Jabo by his throat, and began choking him.

"Boss, I didn't know. I swear I didn't!"

"If you would have killed my son, I would have unloaded a full clip in your face. You better not even think about harming my blood." Brasco pulled out his gun and stuck it to Jabo's temple.

"OK, boss, I got you."

"This is my first and last time I'll tell you this." Then finally, Brasco released his grip.

"Boss, what're we going to do about Freeway? You know how he gets down."

"I don't know, but we definitely got to send a message."

"Hey, boss, you know he still has one stash house in the city," Jabo said.

"I thought he went legit. Didn't he get rid of all his trap houses?"

"Nope, and it's in plain sight where nobody would notice."

"What is it?"

"It's a fucking Laundromat."

"That's one clever motherfucker," Brasco had to admit.

"Get this. He has nobody guarding it because nobody would expect it," Jabo continued.

"Damn, I'm surprised you never robbed it before."

"I mean, it's Freeway's. I didn't want to fuck with that without no help," Jabo explained.

"We about to go hit that right now."

Brasco popped his trunk to see what guns he had on deck.

"Boss, I told you nobody's guarding it," Jabo reminded him.

"I know Freeway. Trust me. He's got somebody in there. He *always* protects his money."

Brasco popped open a black case in his trunk and pulled out a MAC-10. They jumped back into the car. Jabo told him the location, and they drove for about ten blocks before stopping in front of the Laundromat. The first thing Brasco thought was that this Laundromat had too much traffic. "Something is definitely going on in there. Let's go."

They quickly got out of the car. Jabo pulled out his gun and cocked it. Brasco walked in the front of the store with his MAC-10 in the air. Everybody scattered and ran out of the shop. Then Jabo fired his gun, shattering the glass out of the Laundromat door.

Brasco walked up and swung open the door. The lady attendant who gave people change for their dollars for the machines raised her hands. Jabo walked right over to her.

"Bitch, who else in here?" He grabbed her by her long braids.

"They in the back! Please don't kill me."

"How many?"

"There's four of them."

"Get the fuck out of here, and don't come back."

Brasco and Jabo made their way back to the room where the guards were. Finally, they got to the door, and Jabo lightly turned the knob to see if it was open.

"It's locked," he whispered.

"Of course, it's locked, fool." Brasco shook his head at Jabo's stupidity.

"What now?" Jabo asked, ready to make a move.

"Stand back." Brasco aimed his MAC-10 and started shooting through the door.

After that, Jabo kicked it in. The room was so small that two guys got shot and killed instantly by the bullets that breezed through the door. One guy tried to run for the back door, but Jabo shot him. The last guy was too scared to move. He couldn't believe somebody was stupid enough to steal from Freeway.

"You get the fuck over here now," Brasco demanded.

"Do you know whose spot this is?" the man asked.

"Yeah, I know. So that's why you're going to send him a message."

"OK, just don't shoot."

"Tell Freeway I got his money, and now, it's war, bitch." Then he smacked the guy with his gun, knocking him to the floor.

Jabo bagged up all the money that was on the table. Finished, they left the Laundromat with Brasco feeling like he had a little leverage. He wanted to send one final blow to Freeway, so he went back in and shot up the whole store with his weapon. It felt good for Brasco to be back to his old ways. Finally, he felt powerful again. He believed he could compete with Freeway for once. Brasco got back into the car as Jabo threw the money in the backseat.

"Boss, you realize we have done something nobody has ever done?"

"What's that?"

"We robbed Freeway."

They both laughed and felt proud as they pulled off.

Freeway was sitting down eating dinner when he got a call about his shop being robbed. He answered it but couldn't make out what the guy was saying because he was frantic. Finally, Freeway got upset that the guy wasn't talking clearly.

"Speak the fuck up. You messing up my dinner."

"You were robbed, and the Laundromat got shot the fuck up."

"Nigga, is you crazy? Who the fuck would rob me?" Freeway knew people feared him.

"He told me to tell you that he had your money, and now it's war, bitch."

"Where's the rest of the crew that's supposed to guard my shit?"

"They all dead, Freeway. They only left me alive to deliver this message."

"Stay put. You got some explaining to do. I swear on everything I love if you behind this, you will *never* breathe again."

"Freeway, I'm not that stupid to fuck with your money. I don't have a death wish."

Angry, Freeway hung up in the guy's face. Next, he called his daughter. He first thought that her boyfriend stole his money to get even. Since the boy was new in the city, he didn't think anybody else had the guts because no one had tried him in over twenty years.

Calista finally picked up.

"Hey, Dad, wassup?" she sobbed. "Don't fucking 'Hey, Dad' me. Did you and your boyfriend take from me? Calista, you're my daughter, and I love you, but I swear to God if you stole from me—" fussed Freeway.

"What? How dare you! Last night, Kendrick and I fought because I chose you over him. I haven't spoken to him since. I'm in my house crying my eyes out. Dad, why would I steal from you when I can just ask?"

Freeway got quiet as her words rang true. Then pulling on his dreads, he said,

"If you didn't, then your boyfriend did."

"Dad, think about it. He's new here, just like me. Kendrick never heard of you, and he doesn't know where your shit is," said Calista, defending him.

"You might be right," he responded.

"Dad, if he knew who you were, do you think he would have pushed you like that the night at the hospital? Shit, *I'm* your daughter, and *I* don't know a lot about you, but I know you're not to be played with."

"I need you to get him and bring him to me."

"Why would I do that?" Calista didn't trust this.

"I promise I won't do nothing if he's truly innocent. Then his name will be cleared."

"Maybe you should apologize for beating him up too. He was just protecting me."

"We'll see. Bring him to me, please." Freeway hung up the phone and headed to the Laundromat.

Calista had to do the unthinkable and get Kendrick when they didn't see eye to eye. No matter how she felt, she had to get him so that he could clear his name—or she knew her father would kill him. So she put Amari into the car and drove off. The whole ride there, she was preparing herself.

When she got to his mom's house, her heart began to beat fast. She grabbed Amari, headed for the front door, and knocked lightly. After a few seconds, she knocked again only a little harder. Finally, Mona answered the door.

"What the hell are you doing here?" Mona knew she was supposed to apologize, but that went out the window when her son got beat up.

"I need to speak with Kendrick, please."

"Don't you think you and your father have done enough? Your father thinks he's untouchable, but somebody will kill him one day."

"My father doesn't *think* he's untouchable. He *knows* this. He's a *boss*. I love Kendrick, but what happened was *not* my father's fault. Kendrick put his hands on him first."

"Mom, who are you talking to?" Kendrick walked up to the front door.

"Nobody that you need to see."

Kendrick approached the door anyway and was shocked to see Calista. He looked at his mom and assured her it was OK and that he would talk to her one-on-one.

Mona rolled her eyes and went back inside. The two stood silent for a few minutes until Calista jumped right into the real reason she was there.

"My father needs to see you, and I mean like right now." She let it be known it was urgent.

"I should have known. It's all about your father."

"No, Kendrick, you don't understand. He thinks you robbed him."

"Why the fuck would I steal from your father?"

"He thinks you was trying to get even."

"I been here the whole time. I haven't done shit," he said, upset.

"OK, so, please, go clear your name."

"I don't trust your father."

"You have my word that he will not do anything to you once he knows the truth. I don't know much about him, but I have learned he is honest."

"Fine. Let's get this over with."

Kendrick went back into the house to tell his mom that he was leaving and that something important had come up. She didn't like him leaving with Calista, but he was grown. He kissed her and ran out to get in her car. Calista had already called her father and learned he was at the Laundromat. He gave her directions.

When they arrived at the Laundromat, Kendrick got extremely nervous when he saw that Freeway had a guy on the ground and his associate had a gun to the guy's head. Calista didn't want her baby to witness this, and Kendrick understood and went to face Freeway alone.

As Kendrick walked up close, Freeway made his associate pick up the guy and looked at Kendrick's face.

"Is this the guy that robbed you?" Freeway asked, gripping the man's face to focus on Kendrick.

"No, the guy that robbed us had a lot of tattoos, and he used to be the one people feared until you came back into town."

"Brasco . . . *Brasco* fucking robbed me and wants war? Then he'll get what he's asking for."

Chapter 31

Crossroads

"Send him," Freeway said, looking at his associate.

Right in front of Kendrick, the guy got his brains blown out. Kendrick didn't know what to expect next. Freeway had to admit Kendrick had guts just to show up. His associate dragged the dead body to the van they were driving. Freeway was about to give Kendrick the apology he deserved.

"Come over here and let me talk to you."

"You sure we cool?" Kendrick asked as he was so nervous after seeing a man murdered.

"Trust me, if I wanted you dead, you'd already be dead. Now, come here, and don't make me ask you twice."

"Fine." Kendrick walked over.

"Listen, I apologize for what I did to you, but *nobody* puts hands on me." He placed his hand on Kendrick's shoulder.

"I understand. I just thought Calista was with another guy. I would have never done that if I knew you were her father."

"You know what? I like you, kid. You're willing to protect my daughter, and that speaks volumes. Go tell my daughter to come here."

"Sure thing, sir."

"Don't do that," Freeway smirked.

"What's that?"

"Call me, 'sir.' You don't work for me."

"OK, I'll get Calista now." Kendrick walked to the car to let Calista know her father needed her.

He played with Amari in the car. He figured Freeway wanted to have a private moment with his daughter.

Calista looked around to make sure no dead bodies were about. She didn't want to see that shit. The first words out of Freeway's mouth shocked her.

"Fix it."

"Excuse me?"

"You heard what I said. Fix it."

"OK, Dad, but can you elaborate on what you're talking about?" Calista had no idea what he meant.

"Your relationship . . . You need to fix it. He really loves you and wants to protect you."

"I'm not sure if he still wants me."

"Trust me. He still wants you. Now, I need you to bring Amari to me."

"Why?"

"A war is about to start, and I can't have my granddaughter in harm's way, so I hired a woman I bought a day care for to watch her until this shit blows over."

"My daughter will be safe, right?"

"Of course. She's my granddaughter, now come on. Besides, it will give you and Kendrick time to talk. Hurry up. Get Amari. I got shit to do."

Calista went and got Amari from Kendrick. She slowly walked over and handed her to Freeway. Freeway kissed his granddaughter on the cheek. Then he told Calista to call him if she needed him. She hugged her dad and walked off.

"Hey, Kendrick, keep my daughter safe. Call me if shit pops off and stay away from Brasco," Freeway shouted while getting into the van.

"Will do." Kendrick looked at Calista smiling at him. "When the hell did you and my dad become so close?" she said jokingly.

"Hey, we talked and realized we had something in common."

"Yeah, and what was that?"

"Protecting you. I told him that if I knew he was your daddy, I would have never done that."

They both watched as Freeway drove away in the van. He was holding Amari while his associate was driving. They looked at the truck until it faded down the street. Then Calista looked at Kendrick and wrapped her arms around his neck. Their energy was explosive. It was like they had never been separated. They missed each other dearly. Deep in their hearts, they both knew they were done fighting and didn't want ever to do it again. Kendrick kissed her back with passion, and she felt it too.

"Damn, I missed you," he exclaimed.

"You know, even though we were apart, it felt like you were still there." It puzzled Calista.

She didn't have to explain. Kendrick knew precisely what she was talking about because he felt it too. What they shared was very rare. All they knew was they were tired of fighting and wanted to live their life.

"Hey, Kendrick, did you notice something about Brasco?"

"No, what's that?"

"You two resemble each other."

It didn't dawn on him that they did look alike. Was *that* his father? But it couldn't be because his dad had died . . . right? Kendrick knew he had to confront his mother about this. He told Calista to take him to his mother's house so that he could talk to her. He had to ask his mother about his father. They jumped into the car and drove to his mom's house. Once parked, he got out, ran up the steps, and barged in the door.

Mona was happy to see him, but, boy, was she in for a surprise. Calista stayed in the car. She felt like this was a private matter. Plus, she didn't want Kendrick's mom to feel like he was confronting her because she was there.

"Hey, baby."

"Did you lie to me?" Kendrick questioned.

"Boy, what are you talking about now?" she asked.

"Mom, I'm going to ask you this one time, and one time only."

"Kendrick, I don't know what you're talking about."

"Is my father dead?"

"You know what I told you," Mona said, getting nervous.

"Let me put this a different way. Is *Brasco* my father?"

Instantly, Mona broke down crying. This was confirmation for Kendrick that Brasco was indeed his father. Now, he knew why Brasco was so anxious to get at Freeway. He knew Freeway had put his hands on his son. Kendrick couldn't believe his mother had lied all those years. His father had started a war with Freeway, and now, it was a mess.

"You always told me I shouldn't keep secrets or lie, but look what *you* did to me."

"Kendrick, you don't understand. He was in jail for seventeen years, so basically, he *was* dead to us."

"You should have been a woman and told me the truth."

"Kendrick, I'm sorry!" She kept crying.

"So, *he's* the one that really bought the pastry shop—*not* you." Kendrick turned around and walked out of the house. He was furious with his mother.

"Kendrick, come back!" She followed him outside.

"Mom, right now, I need space from you. Some real shit is going on, and my no-good father started it."

"You running the streets is not going to solve nothing. Look, I'm so sorry, baby."

"You constantly saying you're sorry won't fix the issue." Kendrick got in the car and told Calista to drive off.

"Where we going, boo?"

"Go to the pastry shop. Let's just park and talk, OK?"

"Cool. Does Brasco know he's your father?"

"I'm afraid so, but don't worry. I'm on your dad's side." Kendrick felt betrayed by both his parents.

Brasco and Jabo counted the money and put it through a money machine, but Jabo saw that his boss still didn't look like he was celebrating. They had just caught a lick for three million. Who wouldn't be happy right now?

"Boss, come on, man, cheer up. Look what we did."

"Nigga, don't you get it? We took three million from a baller. Freeway's coming for his money, so I got to hit him where he'll be most vulnerable."

"Where would that be, boss?"

"Taking his little bitch."

"I didn't know Freeway had a girlfriend."

"No, I'm talking about his daughter. I'm about to soften up this nigga."

Freeway and Brasco used to be partners until they both realized they wanted to be the boss. They told each other everything. Freeway told Brasco that he left his daughter and her mother because he didn't want anybody to use that love against him. They were friends and partners for a few years. Then, Freeway began to gain too much muscle for Brasco. But Brasco had to admit that while he was partying, Freeway was putting in that work.

Brasco hated the fact that Freeway became much larger than him, but before splitting, Freeway told Brasco he could have Atlanta—but here Freeway was . . . taking over again. Brasco hated how people feared Freeway more than they did him. However, Freeway was extremely dangerous. He would kill with no remorse.

"So, boss, we're going to kidnap that girl, but what about your son?"

"We need to lock him out of the way. Let me handle my son. You get the girl, understand?"

"Loud and clear, boss."

"You said they'd be hanging out at his pastry shop, right?"

"Yeah, that's where I saw her at."

"Well, let's go."

Kendrick and Calista pulled up at the pastry shop and parked the car. She could tell Kendrick was hurt and felt betrayed by the lies his mother told him. Not knowing her father all those years, she understood his pain. She grabbed his hand and kissed it. He finally smiled.

"So, what's it like?" Kendrick asked.

"What you mean?"

"Your dad is well respected, a fucking boss."

"I don't know. I never really thought about it because I don't see him in that light."

"That's understandable. He's your father."

"You act like your father's not ruthless," Calista said.

"You know what? You're right. He killed this guy when I was at the bar. Your father seemed to be with his money and went legit."

It was amazing how these two beautiful spirits came together, and two absent fathers created them. They felt like nothing could separate them again. Kendrick was starting to feel bad about how he left his mother. She still did a good job raising him. Unfortunately, his father chose to do the shit that got him taken away from his family.

"You think I should call my mother?" He wanted advice.

"I would. You see what happened to me. I almost missed my chance to say goodbye. You just never know . . ."

"Yeah, you might be right. I think I'll call her. I know she's worried." He pulled out the phone while getting out of the car. Plus, he had to use the bathroom.

Calista was sitting back listening to some jazz while Kendrick was gone. She was happy that he was back in her life. Their energy was way too strong to be apart. She sure would be glad when everything was calm so she could get her baby back.

Kendrick went into the shop. All the employees waved at him as he walked to the bathroom. He called his mom, who picked up on the first ring. She was so thankful to hear his voice. He smiled as if she could see him.

"Mom, I'm sorry for the way I acted."

"Son, it's OK. You had every right to be mad. I should have never lied to you."

"Mom, he chose to get locked up, and you raised me without him."

"Where are you, son?"

"I'm at the pastry shop." He zipped up his pants as he was leaving the bathroom.

"Before you leave, go in the office and grab that blue folder off the computer for me."

"Sure thing. Mom, I love you."

He went into the office to look for the blue folder. He didn't find a thing, so he decided to look in all the file cabinets. He knew the blue folder contained the price sheets.

Calista closed her eyes, tapping her feet to the beat of the music. She was hoping Kendrick would hurry up. Suddenly, her thoughts were interrupted by the sound of her door being snatched open.

"Remember me, little slick-mouthed bitch?" Jabo dragged her out of the car, smacking her face hard.

While dragging her to their car, Brasco yelled for him to hurry up. Kendrick came running out of the building because he heard screaming. Brasco had no choice but to pull his gun on his son. Jabo threw Calista into the trunk, and as Kendrick charged at Brasco, Brasco hit him in the face with his weapon.

"So, *this* how you treat your son?" Kendrick asked as he wiped the blood from his lip. "So, your sorry ass is my daddy?"

"Oh, she finally told you? Well, son, you tell Freeway I got his little bitch-ass daughter," smirked Brasco. Then they got into the car and drove off.

Kendrick pulled out his phone and called Freeway.

"Hello."

"They fucking got her, Freeway. They kidnapped Calista!"

"Who the fuck got Calista?" Freeway growled.

"Brasco and some other nigga," Kendrick cried.

"You put the streets on notice that the whole Atlanta's going to bleed until I get my baby girl back," Freeway told his top hitta. "What direction were they headed?" he asked Kendrick.

"They headed toward Springfield Missionary," Kendrick answered.

"Let me get on the horn and hit up my crew to be on the lookout," said Freeway.

"They're in a black Dodge Charger," added Kendrick.

"Where are you at?" Freeway asked.

"I'm at Kendrick's Pastry."

"I'm on my way," Freeway told him.

"All right," Kendrick replied and hung up.

Minutes later, Freeway had woken up the streets, alerting everyone to be on the lookout. There was a $200,000 bounty placed on Brasco and Jabo's heads.

"We can't find them standing around. Let's ride," barked Freeway.

Brasco and Jabo turned on High Point Trails and slowly drove around the winding road as colonial homes started to line both sides.

"Aye, man, we have to ditch this car," said Brasco.

Jabo spoke up. "Where the fuck are we headed? You know Freeway's got every motherfucker in the city looking for us by now."

Brasco swiped his face and tugged at his beard. "My cousin lives at the end of this street. We'll swap cars with him and get the fuck out of Dodge," he frowned. Both men were visibly concerned.

"That blue house there, pull around the back," barked Brasco.

"A'ight. Chill, nigga." Jabo scowled as he pulled into the long driveway.

The driveway opened into a big backyard with two metal buildings used as a body and paint shop.

"Ayeee, cuzzo," yelled Brasco.

Jabo blew the horn.

Seconds later, a tall, dark, older man sauntered out wearing grey coveralls. His aged face was covered by a long, thick beard and a cigar hanging from his lips.

"Why y'all sum of a bitches making so much noise outchea?" he fussed.

"Cuz, I'm in a tight bind. I need you, boy," said Brasco as he nervously tugged at his beard.

Frank wiped his sweaty face with his handkerchief, then asked, "What's in it for me?"

"Man, your people on some bullshit," Jabo complained.

*Boom*Boom*Boom* distracted their conversation.

"What the fuck y'all got in the trunk?" Frank frowned and side-eyed Brasco and Jabo.

"Cuz, I need a switch out," Brasco said, ignoring Frank's question.

"Bruh, wassup? This nigga the police or some shit?" Jabo asked, who was now leaning over the hood of the car.

"Nah, don't know what shit y'all got going on, and I don't want no parts of it," Frank said, waving them away.

Jabo stood up and started counting out money. "How much to get some shit shaking?"

"Bruh, I don't want none of this trouble. So y'all need to scatter," Frank told them as he looked away.

Seconds later, his phone rang. "This Frank," he answered.

"Yeah, come on through," he said before ending the call.

Jabo looked at Brasco with sweat rolling down his face.

"Bruh, this nigga on some bullshit. Let's roll."

"See you, cuz. I'm out," said a disappointed Brasco. As he headed to get back into the car, Calista thumped louder in the trunk.

Jabo walked to the back of the car with his gun drawn.

"Yooo, chill with whatever shit you about to do," barked Frank as he slid out his 9 mm.

"Cuz, I got this," Brasco said as he pushed Jabo in the chest.

"What the fuck, nigger?" scowled Brasco standing over Jabo with his 38. snub nose aimed.

The crackling of the gravel made everyone freeze. Brasco knew his getaway plan had been foiled.

An Audi A7 quickly pulled in, catching Brasco off guard. Freeway jumped out with Kendrick behind him. A black Chevy work van followed them.

"So, you motherfuckers were dumb enough to touch my most prized possession?" he frowned as he pointed his MAC-10 at Brasco.

"Good looking out, Frank," said Freeway.

"Open the motherfucking trunk," he ordered.

Kendrick finally spoke. "Did he stutter? Throw the fucking keys."

Jabo tossed him the keys, and he popped the trunk. Calista was lying there, covered with sweat and grime from the filthy interior of the trunk. Kendrick helped her out.

"Damn, I'm glad to see you," smiled Calista.

Kendrick pulled her into a tight hug. "I know. You're my fucking world," he responded.

Six men from the van stood holding semiautomatic guns.

"You know you fucked up, right?" said Freeway.

He quickly let off a round, hitting Jabo in the forehead. Blood splattered, and his head exploded on impact. Instantly, his body slumped as blood spurted out of the stump that was his head.

"Damn, that made a mess," Frank joked. "That will be extra for cleanup."

"I could give a shit about the money, but you made that shit real personal," Freeway said to Brasco.

"It wasn't personal. But you know the game," Kendrick stuttered as he let off a round striking Brasco in the chest.

The impact knocked him to the ground.

"Now, *this* is personal, motherfucker. You broke my mother's heart and kidnapped my bae," said Kendrick, pointing the gun at Brasco's head.

"Yo, little punk ass won't kill me." But Brasco flinched as Kendrick squeezed the trigger, knocking his body back.

"Motherfucker, your time is up," smirked Kendrick.Calista ran to him and pulled him into a comforting hug.

"Damn, youngblood, I'm impressed," Freeway smirked as the six men from the van quickly cleaned up the remnants of Jabo and Brasco.

"I know that was your fam, Frank, but he was on some snake shit," Freeway said as he handed him four envelopes full of money.

"Excuse my language and all, but fuck him. It was just his Karma giving back to him," Frank commented.

"I'll wire the rest as soon as I get situated," Freeway said as Frank sprayed down his yard.

"You have always looked out for me," Frank admitted.

"Let's head out," said Freeway.

"Hey, boss, you might want these," said one of the cleanup crew members.

Freeway turned on his heels and saw six duffel bags at his hitta's feet.

"They were in the trunk," he informed him.

"Take two and split it with Frank and your guys. Take the other four back to the shop. Crisp that car. Leave no traces," ordered Freeway.

Calista and Kendrick were waiting in the car. Freeway smiled to himself as he sauntered back toward them. Minutes later, the shop area was spotless. The cleanup crew left no traces . . .